MEET T[...]
THE CINE[...]

Our Hero, Roger Gordo[...] [...] for old movies was matched only by his passion for the mysterious Delores.

The Sidekick, Big Louie—His fascination for evil was matched only by his inability to be truly mean.

The Town Drunk, Doc—His thirst for hard liquor was matched only by the strength of his liver.

The Beauty, Delores—Her will to survive was matched only by her desire for a black vinyl jump suit.

The Arch-Fiend, Doctor Dread—His desire for total destruction was matched only by his lack of good taste.

The Mysterious Man in White—His gleaming acts of courage were matched only by his gleaming white wardrobe.

DON'T MISS THESE OTHER HILARIOUS SERIES BY CRAIG SHAW GARDNER... *THE EBENEZUM TRILOGY* AND *THE BALLAD OF WUNTVOR*

"A lot of fun! I could hardly wait to find out what was going to happen next!"
—**Christopher Stasheff,**
author of *The Warlock Insane*

"A delight for all fans of funny fantasy!"
—**Will Shetterly,**
author of *Cats Have No Lords*

"A slapstick romp worthy of Laurel & Hardy...but I warn you not to read it late at night—the neighbors will call the cops when you laugh down the walls!"
—**Marvin Kaye,**
author of *The Incredible Umbrella*

CRAIG SHAW GARDNER

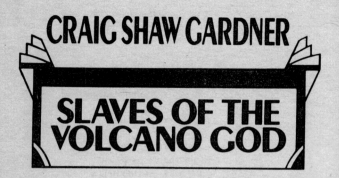

SLAVES OF THE VOLCANO GOD

ACE BOOKS, NEW YORK

This book is an Ace original edition,
and has never been previously published.

SLAVES OF THE VOLCANO GOD

An Ace Book/published by arrangement with
the author

PRINTING HISTORY
Ace edition/October 1989

ISBN: 0-441-76977-2

Ace Books are published by The Berkley Publishing Group,
200 Madison Avenue, New York, New York 10016.
The name "ACE" and the "A" logo are trademarks
belonging to Charter Communications, Inc.

PRINTED IN THE UNITED STATES OF AMERICA

10 9 8 7 6 5 4 3 2 1

This book is for the two Toms;
Count von Eins bis Zwei
and
the *other* Bad Movie Commando.

CHAPTER

1

Roger thought he should be able to deal with anything. He worked in public relations, after all. He prided himself on facing crises.

"I told you not to move," the man in the trench coat reiterated. The man's voice was almost theatrically gruff. Roger might have found this whole thing funny if the man had not been waving such a large gun in Roger's direction. And he had been waving that gun for an awfully long time. Some crises, Roger reflected, were worse than others.

Perhaps if he worked in public relations out in the business world, rather than in a cloistered university setting, he might be better able to cope with a gun. Still, he didn't think guns showed up in the world of business public relations either. At least, not very often.

The whole thing had, of course, begun with Delores. Ah, Delores! Just thinking of her slim form and long, blond hair, her full lips, her eyes as blue as the Caribbean, Roger wanted to swoon.

He stopped himself immediately. Swooning, as far as Roger knew, was a form of moving. The man with the gun was not too keen on moving. He had mentioned this to Roger many times. Could something go on this long and still be considered a crisis?

"Oh, Roger," Delores had said in her husky voice, as distinctive in its way as the voice of the man with the trench coat. Then Delores had kissed him—the kind of kiss that starts on the lips but somehow manages to work its way down to the toes. "My Roger," she had said as she tousled his sandy brown hair, and with those words, he had known his fate was sealed. He was "her Roger," and he knew what happened when Delores really wanted something. After all, if she hadn't attacked that vending machine, he never would have met her in the first place.

What really surprised Roger, however, was the equal certainty that he considered this woman "his Delores." After what had happened to him with Susan, he had never thought he could feel this way about a woman again. Heaven knows, he never felt the same way when he walked into a supermarket. But somehow, supermarkets no longer seemed important. They were "her Roger" and "his Delores"; that was what was important. And that was it, no matter what.

"No moving," the man in the trench coat said again. He paused. "Well, I suppose you can smile. I mean, we all have to move some, don't we? You can't help but blink your eyes. That sort of thing. But no big movements. I think that's what the guys meant. I wonder what's taking them so long?"

"Guys?" Roger asked. Somehow, this was all beginning to seem like some particularly bad *film noir*.

"No talking now!" The man in the trench coat waved the gun even more in Roger's direction than he had before. "Smiling's okay, but talking's definitely out. Talking is moving, and then some! I know my orders. You tell Big Louie to do something, he does it!"

Big Louie? The guy with the gun wasn't any more than five foot four, and one time when the floor-length trench coat swung open, Roger could have sworn he glimpsed elevator shoes. Just what was going on here?

"Just what's going on here?" the little man in the trench coat whined as if he had read Roger's mind. "Those guys should be here by now. I mean, this is where Delores lives, isn't it?"

Roger cleared his throat. "Well—" he began.

Roger found the gun pressed against his nose.

"What did I say about talking?" Big Louie hissed. He frowned and removed the gun from Roger's nostril. "Well, I suppose you can talk if you're answering a question. That's only fair, isn't it?" The gunman shrugged. "I'm a little new at this. I hope it isn't too obvious."

The gunman lapsed into silence, and Roger once again thought about Delores. So beautiful, so witty, so full of life. There had to be a catch. That's one thing Roger had learned in his thirty-two years upon this Earth. There was always a catch.

"There's always a catch," Big Louie mumbled, more to himself than to Roger. "Hey, they say to me, you want a chance at the big time? Sure, I says. Okay, they say, we got a job for you, a piece of cake. I'll do it, I says, but I have to have a gang-type name. What's wrong with Seymour? they ask. Hey, I says, if I'm gonna do gang things, I gotta fit the part. What's wrong with Seymour? they ask. Seymour, they continue, is a perfectly good name. You know the type. They never understand the important things!" Louie came out of his slouch to stand as tall as he was able. Yes, he was definitely wearing elevator shoes. "I want to be called Big Something, I says. Like Big Seymour? they ask." Big Louie sighed. "You know the type. They never understand." The gunman slouched again, lapsing into gloomy silence.

Roger wondered if he could risk saying something. He had given up trying to overcome the short gunman—heck, he had even given up thinking about it—approximately ten seconds after Big Louie had arrived. The short fellow was too quick, and, even worse, too nervous. Plus, this gangster had caught Roger in his jogging suit.

There was something about wearing a set of navy blue sweats, even the fancy kind with the white stripes down the pants. Whether it was that he was caught without a belt, or that—he had to admit it—his stomach wasn't quite as flat as it should be, being in a jogging suit made Roger feel somehow—how should he put it?—particularly vulnerable. Especially when he was looking into the barrel of a gun. Roger had to face it: He was a runner, not a fighter.

He paused for a long moment, waiting for the man in the trench coat to make a move, but Big Louie did nothing but sigh and stare moodily at his gun.

"Did you want me to answer a question?" Roger asked at last.

"What?" Big Louie started, gun at the ready. "What did I tell you—oh, that's right—I did. Yeah. I guess so. I mean, with the guys not showing up and all, I guess we have to change the rules a little." He lowered his weapon. "So, let me ask you. Just where is Delores?"

Roger told him she had left half an hour before.

"What?" The little guy shook his gun in disbelief. "You mean she's already gone? That would be just like those guys. A piece of cake, they say." The small man shook with fury. He pointed his revolver straight at Roger's stomach. His knuckles were white where he held his gun.

"There's only one thing I want to know," Big Louie whispered between clenched teeth. "What am I waiting around here for?"

The gunman vanished in a puff of blue smoke.

Roger blinked.

Did this mean the crisis was over?

The first thing Roger was aware of was lips. And what lips! Only one woman in the world kissed like that.

"Delores!" Roger gasped when she let him come up for air. At least she was safe! He had been so worried about her after the short gunman had shown up. It was only natural, after all, especially since that incident between Roger and Dierdre—although in that case it had been a rifle, not a revolver. And there had been that overripe avocado, too. But he had promised himself he wasn't going to think about Dierdre anymore, or Susan, or Wanda, or—well, he especially wasn't going to think about Phyllis! All that sort of thing was over, now that he'd met Delores.

But Delores hadn't told him where she was going. She was like that. Roger really thought she enjoyed being mysterious. This time, though, her sense of mystery might have been fatal. Even if he had known whether or not he should warn her about Big Louie, there was no way he could have gotten in touch with her.

So eventually he had exchanged his jogging suit for a pair of striped pajama pants and crawled into bed. Even more eventually, he had fallen asleep. None of his real dreams had come close to Big Louie. That had worried him even more. Just what was Delores mixed up in?

She put a finger to her lips. His dreams had gone away, replaced by Delores' magnificent reality.

"Have they been here?" she whispered. Roger always had to be careful not to shiver when she whispered.

He nodded.

"I was afraid of that." Delores frowned. "I really didn't want to get you mixed up in this, Roger." She sighed wistfully. Roger loved it when she sighed wistfully. "It's a little late for that now, though."

She stroked his bare shoulder tentatively. "I think I should tell you everything. But I will have to hurry. I don't think we have much time."

She looked around the room, as if she expected someone to pop out of nowhere at any second. Roger remembered Big Louie and the blue smoke. Satisfied that they were alone for the moment, Delores reached into the pocket of her black vinyl jump suit and took out a small, shiny object. She pressed the object into Roger's hand.

"This is what they were after," she said.

Roger studied the strangely familiar object in the bedroom's dim light. He held a hollow silver-colored oval, made of some lightweight plastic, with an insignia attached to one end. It looked like nothing so much as a Captain Crusader Decoder Ring.

Roger remembered Captain Crusader Decoder Rings from his childhood. You got one whenever you bought a box of Nut Crunchies. You needed them to understand the messages written in Captain Crusader's secret codes that always appeared on the back of the box.

He could still remember decoding those messages on his breakfast napkins: "Civic Responsibility is everybody's business." "Every day starts better with a smile." "Always look both ways before you cross the street." Roger had always wondered what was so special about those messages that they had to be written in code. Still, anything that came for free in a box of Nut Crunchies was worth saving, and Roger would always keep the rings. At one time, he had had seven.

He looked back at the object in his hand. "What is it?" he asked, afraid in his heart she would tell him it was a Captain Crusader Decoder Ring.

"This," Delores intoned solemnly, "is the key to the universe."

"Oh," Roger replied. Actually, he didn't like that answer much more than the one he had anticipated. This tiny, cheap, plastic thing was the key to the universe? He turned on his overhead reading light to better study the small, silver-colored band. It still looked just like a Captain Crusader Decoder Ring.

"Actually," Delores confessed, "it's a Captain Crusader Decoder Ring." She smiled one of her dazzling Delores smiles. "But the people at Nut Crunchies never realized what they had wrought with the invention of this little marvel." She winked at Roger. "You see, you can use this little ring to go anywhere you want in the Cineverse, to any one of those uncounted million worlds—"

"Hold it!" Roger cried. This was all too complicated. After that mess he had gotten in with Vicki, Roger had sworn off complicated relationships once and for all. At least he thought he had.

"Whatever is going on here," Roger continued, "you have to start your explanation from the beginning." He pointed at the piece of plastic in his other hand. "I do not believe a Captain Crusader Decoder Ring qualifies as a beginning."

Delores pouted. "Well, it is." Lord, Roger thought, Delores was beautiful when she pouted! "At least," she continued, "it is in a way. Well, actually, it's a very complicated beginning. Maybe there's some other way I can explain."

Her frown only lasted a few seconds. She snapped her fingers and smiled.

"Roger," she said, "you really like to go to the movies, don't you?"

Roger looked at her in astonishment. That was like asking him if he liked to breathe. Just the night before, he had taken Delores to see a triple feature of jungle action pictures at the local revival house: *Zabana, Prince of the Jungle*, *Zabana Versus the Nazi Death Ray*, and *Zabana Goes to Hollywood*. And she asked him if he liked movies!

"Well, yes," he answered after a moment's pause.

With that, Delores once again showed her fabulous smile. "I know you do, darling. Your love of movies is a big part of why we're involved. That surprises you, doesn't it? I suppose I should have told you about all this sooner. Still, our romance was so perfect." Her cool fingers ran across his knuckles. She chuckled ruefully. "It was almost like a movie."

Her touch sent waves of chill excitement down Roger's spine. Maybe he was being too hard on Delores. After all, complications had a way of sneaking up on you, especially in relationships. There was nothing Delores and he couldn't work out somehow. Especially when they were alone together. Somehow, as Delores spoke, she seemed closer and closer to him, and Big Louie and the blue smoke seemed farther and farther in the distance.

"Not now, Roger!" Delores gently pushed him away. "Oh, I want to, too, but we don't have time when the fate of the universe is at stake!"

Her frown deepened as she continued to speak: "You know quite a bit about movies, films made thirty, forty, even fifty years ago." She paused again, and bit her lip. "Well, what if I were to tell you that those movies were more than just movies?"

"What?" Roger asked. Somehow, the more Delores explained, the more confusing this became.

Delores took a deep breath. "Let me tell you the whole thing. I think that would be best. Please don't interrupt. You can ask me questions when I'm done."

She sat down next to him on the bed. "There are many other worlds, Roger, worlds not so different from the one that contains this room, this bed, and the two of us. Actually, Roger, you would find these other worlds strangely familiar. For you have seen these worlds in the movies!"

"In the movies?" Roger whispered.

"Roger," Delores reprimanded, "your interjections are not helping. Just listen." She nodded her head emphatically. "That's right. For a time, Hollywood, U.S.A. had managed to tap into the universal subconscious, and was showing this world—your world, Roger, not mine— glimpses of the Cineverse."

"The Cineverse?" Roger queried.

Delores' lovely frown deepened. "Roger. Please. I am trying to use terms that you will comprehend. I'm talking about the almost infinite number of worlds that occupy this same space in all the many universes. That was what Hollywood had keyed into, at least until *the Change!*"

"The Change?" Roger inquired.

She nodded emphatically. "Yes. The Change. It must have been obvious, especially to someone with a background like yours. I mean, you must have noticed that movies aren't as good as they used to be."

Roger paused. She was right. Movies *weren't* as good as they used to be. He felt a chill at the pit of his stomach. Maybe there was really some truth to all this stuff she was spouting!

"Now, this is all serious enough, but I haven't told you about the real danger." Her frown deepened. Three worry lines creased her lovely forehead. "I know this must be confusing to you. Maybe it would be better to show you. Roger, could I please have the ring?"

Roger handed it over in silence.

"Here," she said, squeezing Roger's hand as she took

the ring away. "Let me show you how to open a window to the beyond." She held the ring under the light. "First, you turn the Captain Crusader Decoder Dial—"

There was a puff of blue smoke, accompanied by the usual low-key explosion. Delores leapt to her feet and screamed.

"Heeheeheehahahaha!"

The room was filled with hideous laughter. A voice cried: "We knew you'd have to activate that thing eventually!"

The smoke took some time to clear. When Roger stopped coughing, he saw they had been joined by four figures. One of them was Big Louie. He and two others were wearing double-breasted suits straight out of some bad Prohibition era film.

But the other man's costume was something else altogether. He was wearing long robes—and hat to match—of the deepest black, made more striking still by the bright red stitching upon the sleeves, stitching that formed shapes that almost—but not quite—looked like letters or words. For an instant, Roger wondered if these shapes might be ancient symbols of some long-dead language. Then again, perhaps they were only letters and words attempted by someone who wasn't very good at embroidery.

The red squiggles danced around the hat as well, a circular cap that came to a point at the top, except the point was a bit askew, as if the hat might have been sat on once or twice. Roger stared at the hat and discovered that if he squinted, the symbols there looked even more like words. He frowned as he concentrated on the embroidered scrawl, forming the syllables silently with his lips as he read:

DAD'S . . . THE . . . CHEF

"What do you mean, 'Dad's the Chef'?" the fellow in black demanded, his frown accentuated by a severely trimmed mustache. "Unless . . ."

His frown deepened as he glanced down at his apparel.

And, what, Roger wondered, was the meaning of that apparel? The fellow's companions were all dressed as 1930's gangsters, but the man in the black costume came from another era entirely. Roger could swear he had seen that kind of conical cap before somewhere. Wasn't it the sort of thing schoolchildren were forced to wear when they sat in corners after they misbehaved? Yes, it did look rather like a dunce cap. Except the rest of the costume didn't look schoolboyish at all. The robes looked more like the fellow had stepped out of a low budget King Arthur movie. That was it! All he needed was a magic wand, and he'd look just like—

Roger shook his head. A wizard? Could it be possible? The fellow had thrown his hands over his chest, as if he might hide the robes behind them. From this guy's behavior so far, Roger decided he would vote for the dunce theory over the wizard any day.

"Oops," the man in the maybe-a-wizard's outfit apologized as he waved distractedly at his garb. "What am I doing in this? It's totally inappropriate." The fellow's smile was the slightest bit sheepish. "They must have made some sort of mistake in Central Casting. Excuse me, won't you? I shan't be a minute!"

The blue smoke showed up again as the man-who-shouldn't-have-been-a-wizard disappeared. Unfortunately, Big Louie and the other two chose to stick around, menacing Delores and Roger with their snub-nosed .38's.

And then there was another of those all-too-frequent explosions. The voice began to speak even before the blue smoke cleared:

"Sorry for the delay. Now where were we? Oh, yes."

The voice cleared its throat.

"Heeheeheehahahaha!"

The room was once again filled with hideous laughter as the smoke dissipated, and the formerly-dressed-in-black fellow stood before them again, in a costume Roger thought looked even stranger than the last one.

The laugher wore a loose green garment, sort of like an oversize smoking jacket made of some shiny, almost metallic material, with pants to match. The jacket had a large blood-red *D* embroidered on the lapel. And the laughter upon his lips was now replaced by a sardonic smile as he spoke again:

"And now," he began slowly, "we shall get down to what—ahem—really matters."

The man in green removed something from his head that looked vaguely like a space helmet. Actually, Roger reflected, what it most looked like was a fish bowl with a television antenna stuck on top.

"De-lor-ess," the man in green hissed. "You didn't really think fleeing to Earth would save you?" His smile broadened as he examined the woman's form, from blond hair to jump suit to dark black boots. His eyes seemed to glint evilly, but perhaps that was just the reflection of his metallic green suit. He threw his head back to laugh again.

Delores stared angrily at the man in green. "I had no thought of being saved," she whispered between clenched teeth. "What is happening to our worlds is more important than either you or I!"

One of the green man's henchmen spoke up: "What should we do with them, Doctor Dread?"

The green man's smile grew even wider than before. "We will—heh, heh, heh—deal with both of them, if you get my meaning."

The henchman smiled. "Yeah, Doctor Dread. I get your meaning."

Roger was afraid that he got the man in green's meaning as well. Especially since two of the henchpeople were using this opportunity to brandish their large, nasty-looking guns in Delores's and his general direction.

A moment later Big Louie glanced at his fellows and hastily began to wave his gun as well.

It was then that Roger remembered he was only wearing his pajama pants. He felt even more vulnerable than he had in his jogging suit. He sucked his stomach in. How could he possibly save Delores if he wasn't dressed for it? He wondered if he should at least start by getting out of bed. He took another look at the revolvers. He thought better of it.

"Delores," Doctor Dread murmured. Roger couldn't

take his eyes off the man's suit. When the light hit it just right, it looked like snakeskin. "Pretty, pretty Delores," he continued. "You will of course be coming with us." His smile broadened again. "But then, I know how much you like to"—he paused meaningfully—"travel."

"Yeah," one of the henchpeople smiled. "Travel!"

"You idiot!" Delores replied. "How can you think of your own petty plans at a time like this!"

"Hehhehheh," Dread laughed. "My plans are anything but petty. Soon I shall *rule*, but—hehheh—perhaps I say too much. We will discuss this when we are in more private surroundings. Won't we, boys?"

The two henchpeople laughed. Big Louie laughed a second later. The others looked at him.

"Uh," Big Louie said. "Yeah, private surroundings. Yeah—uh—don't say too much. Uh—" Big Louie wiped his forehead. "Uh—What do you want to do with the other guy?"

"I'm glad you brought that up," Doctor Dread remarked. "The other guy, as you so quaintly put it, will have to be—heeheehee—taken care of."

The two other henchpeople laughed. Big Louie tried to join them but the noise died in his throat.

"Taken care of?" Big Louie asked.

"Yes, taken care of." Doctor Dread ran a perfectly manicured hand through his close-cropped hair. "You know." He frowned, and looked at Roger. "What is your name?"

Roger told him.

"Very good." The Doctor's smile returned. "Roger, here, then, must be taken care of. Roger must be"—he paused to chortle—"dealt with. Roger must be—hahahaha—removed from active consideration." Doctor Dread sighed. "I ask you: How can I be any plainer?"

Big Louie swallowed hard. "Removed from active consideration?"

Doctor Dread nodded. "You want to be called Big Louie, you've got to act Big Louie. When you're finished, we'll meet you back"—Dread paused to look suspiciously about the room—"at the usual place.

"Heh, heh, heh. Grab the girl!" Dread ordered a henchman. "And get the ring. And may I say, Roger, that I enjoyed my"—he paused again, his smile a mixture of
supreme triumph and ultimate evil—"final visit?"

Doctor Dread placed the antennaed goldfish bowl over
his head as his henchmen dragged the struggling Delores to
his side. His laughter echoed in the room until the blue
smoke cleared.

Roger stared at Big Louie. More specifically, Roger
stared at the gun shaking along with Louie's right hand.
What was this guy going to do with him?

"What am I going to do with you?" Big Louie asked. He
gripped the shaking gun with his left hand as well, and
pointed it straight at Roger's forehead.

"Sorry," Louie said. "You heard those guys. This is a
part of my job."

Roger yelled and tried to leap for the small man's gun.
He might have made it, too, if he had not been so tangled
up in his bedclothes. It was very difficult to be a hero when
you had a blanket wrapped around your legs.

"You're not making this any easier, are you?" Louie
wailed. He pushed Roger back on the bed. "A minute ago,
I was looking for a way out of this. But I'm afraid you
don't give me any choice!"

Roger felt the cold muzzle of the gun on his too warm
forehead.

"Buddy," the other man whispered hoarsely, "you just
made Big Louie everything he knew he had to be."

CHAPTER

2

"Everything I knew I had to be," Louie added. "Like a complete failure."

Roger felt the gun leave his forehead.

"I just can't do it." Louie stuck the handgun back in his shoulder holster. "Heaven knows I tried. All these years, working in comedy relief. I wanted a break, you know? I thought I could be a henchman." He laughed bitterly as he rebuttoned his coat. "I guess I just wasn't meant to hench."

"Does this mean—" Roger asked cautiously, "that you're not going to kill me?"

"I'm afraid so," Louie said glumly. "Don't spread it around, okay?" The small man paused, a half smile struggling to overcome his frown.

"Wait a second! While I'm bouncing around from world to world with my ring, you're stuck back here on Earth! There's no way anyone will know if I killed you or not!" He giggled. "Fool around with Big Louie, will you?" he pointed a finger at Roger. "Bang, bang, you're dead. Now, if you'll excuse me, I have a date with an evil genius." Big Louie reached in his right-hand pants pocket and frowned.

"Wait!" Roger cried. He couldn't let Big Louie go. Not yet! No matter what nonsense this fellow was spouting, Louie had a Captain Crusader Decoder Ring. Even though Roger still wasn't quite sure what those rings did, he did know one thing: He must get hold of one if he were to ever see Delores again!

"I'll make a deal with you," Roger said hurriedly.

"A deal?" Big Louie pulled his hand from his pocket. The frown was still there.

"Yeah, a deal!" Roger tried to think fast. He had to do it, for Delores! "Let's see. What would someone like you want?" Roger glanced feverishly around his bedroom. There were his color TV, his stereo, his clock radio. Somehow none of this seemed appropriate. "Give me a second! I'll come up with something!"

Louie sighed. "This is what happens when you let somebody live. You want me to make a decision? Hench-people aren't supposed to make decisions. They're just supposed to blindly enact the plans of the evil genius." He pulled something from his breast pocket. Louie allowed himself a little smile. It was a Decoder Ring! "It's my own fault, I suppose. If I had killed you, I wouldn't have to listen to any of this."

"Wait a moment!" Roger blurted. "You haven't heard my offer!" What would a five-foot-high man in double-breasted blue serge want? There certainly wasn't anything here. Roger thought about those golf clubs he had stored at his mother's, the ones Fiona had given him and he had never used. Then there was his old guitar. Sure, the neck was a little warped, but did Big Louie need to know?

"Sorry," the henchman said. "Deals are out. I couldn't do it, no matter how good it was. Let me explain." He held the gray piece of plastic under Roger's nose. "This ring belongs to Doctor Dread. If I should lose it—" Louie made an unpleasant noise deep in his throat as his little finger slashed the air in front of his Adam's apple. "In other words," he continued, a slight harshness in his voice, "I would be taken care of."

Roger thought of Doctor Dread. He swallowed hard. "You mean you'd be dealt with?"

"Yeah." Big Louie nodded. "That's it. Dealt with."

"So they're that valuable?" Roger asked, a hint of wonder in his voice.

Louie nodded. "I only know of three of these things in working order. They break all the time. What do you expect? They're only made out of cheap plastic!"

Roger shook his head. "And these *really* are the key to the universe?"

"Sure are." Louie placed the ring on his finger. "Really says something about the nature of our universe, doesn't it? Well, it's been a lot of fun shooting the breeze, but you'll have to excuse me. I'm expected at the hideout."

Big Louie squinted at the ring, ready to make some fine adjustment with his free hand. The truth sank into Roger's brain at last: This small henchman was going back to Delores, and leaving Roger behind!

"Um—uh—" Roger tried to think of something to say.

"Hemming and hawing won't do you any good," Louie remarked. "No, no. Clearing the throat and coughing isn't any better. I'm leaving, and you're staying here. The only reason you're not dead is that you don't have a ring. Without one of these Captain Crusader numbers, you're not going anyplace!"

Big Louie carefully twisted the dial halfway around. "See you in the funny papers!" he cried. And with that, he was gone.

By now, Roger had gotten quite tired of all this blue smoke. Still coughing, he opened a window to clear the room.

Roger sat back on the bed, atop the blankets that had almost been his undoing. He couldn't give in to despair. There had to be some way he could still reach his beloved.

According to Louie, without a ring, Roger was stuck on Earth forever, Delores eternally beyond his grasp. But, in a moment of panic, Roger had thought of his mother. More specifically, he had thought of his mother's basement.

If things were as he remembered them, Roger did have

a ring. In fact, at one point, he had had seven.

Roger looked at the middle of the room, where he had seen Big Louie and Doctor Dread and Delores all disappear. He jumped out of bed, grabbing the jogging suit he had thrown over a chair the night before.

There was no time to lose!

"Why, Roger, what a surprise!" His mother's smile vanished as he rushed past her and headed for the basement.

"Is my old stuff where I left it?" he called over his shoulder.

"Well—" his mother considered, "I guess so. At least what's left of it."

What's left of it? Roger didn't like the sound of that in the least.

"Aren't you even going to stop and say hello?" his mother called after him.

"Don't have time now, Mom!" Roger shouted as he took the basement steps three at a time. "This is something of an emergency!"

His mother followed him down the steps.

"Where is it?" Roger screamed. Nothing was where it should be! He opened the door on what should have been a fruit cellar and one hundred square feet of boxed storage. Instead, he saw a brightly lit recreation room.

"There's no need to shout, dear." His mother smiled cordially. Roger noticed through his panic that her hair had changed to blond again. "If you'd make yourself clearer, I might be able to answer you. Where is what?"

"All the storage space!" Roger shouted. No, he thought, it didn't do any good to raise your voice when you were around Mother. In a more controlled voice he added: "All those boxes full of stuff from my childhood."

"Oh," his mother said brightly, "those old things? We moved those things out months ago to make room for this new den here. Mr. Mengeles, the nice man next door, has been helping me with home improvements."

She giggled coquettishly. "I hope Mr. Mengeles will help me with everything, pretty soon. Still, dear, if you came over to the house more often, you'd probably notice when I made major changes." She lightly touched Roger's elbow. "Not that I'm criticizing you, dear."

"I don't care if you criticize me or not," Roger replied, doing his best not to shout. "What have you done with my things?"

"You didn't want those old things anymore, did you, dear? As I used to say to Vicki, 'If you let Roger have his way, he'll clutter the house up with all manner of junk!'" She patted her son gently on the shoulder. "Of course, dear, we let you do it because we love you, although heaven knows what value you place in a lot of those things you collect!"

"Mother!" Roger counted silently to ten before he continued. His mother waited patiently for him to finish. Not only had she redone her hair, Roger realized, but she was wearing very stylish clothes in the middle of the day. What was going on here?

"Is Mr. Mengeles coming over?" Roger asked.

His mother blushed. "How did you know?" She smoothed imaginary wrinkles out of her cotton print dress. "You know, dear, I'm always glad to see you, although I wish sometimes that you'd call me before you came here. That's of course assuming that you still know how to use the telephone. Not that I'm criticizing you, dear, but you used to be so much better about keeping in touch when you were married to Susan."

"Mother," Roger interrupted, trying to stop the inevitable. "I do not wish to talk about Susan!"

"And why not?" she chided. "She was always such a nice girl. I don't understand why you ever broke up with Susan, anyway. She let you keep just about anything in that house of yours. Heaven knows it looked like it, with all the clutter everywhere—"

"Mother!" Roger had started to shout again. This was all too much. "I didn't dump Susan, she dumped me! Remember? Susan ran away with the guy who ran the meat counter at the Superette."

"Oh, that's right." A little half smile lit his mother's

countenance. "I remember that fellow." She sighed. "The way he used to say, in that great deep voice of his, 'And would you like that wrapped, madam?' Susan was such a romantic. You didn't deserve her, Roger."

"No, mother, I didn't. Now, what happened to all the boxes?"

"Oh, don't worry, dear, they're around here somewhere. I think Mr. Mengeles put most of them back in this closet." She fluttered across the room in her high heels. "Mr. Mengeles is so handy to have around, dear, and so considerate!"

She reached a door at the back of the room. "I think you'll find almost everything in here," she said as she opened the door. "Oh, of course, I gave all your old comic books to Mr. Mengeles. He has this grand-nephew, Ralph, who just loves comic books. And I must admit that I used most of the stamps from your collection to mail letters. And there's one or two things that I gave away to rummage sales. But, besides that, everything's just as you left it!"

Roger wanted to scream, but he didn't have time. His mother had given away half his childhood!

He looked inside the closet. There were only half a dozen boxes left, out of the thirty or forty he had put here for safekeeping. But so what if his *Tom Corbett*, *Space Cadet* books were gone forever. Roger had to remain calm. There could still be a Captain Crusader Decoder Ring in those boxes that remained!

"Is there a light in here?" he asked.

"There's a pull string overhead," his mother replied. "Mr. Mengeles put that in too. He's so handy to have around."

Roger pulled the string and got to work. The first box was filled with books, the second with old school papers and projects. He took a second to shuffle between his kindergarten drawings and his second-grade science project: "Colors in Nature." He was eating Nut Crunchies in the second grade, wasn't he?

Somewhere, in the distance, a bell rang.

"Oh, dear," his mother said. "It's been awfully nice

seeing you, dear, but I'm afraid you'll have to go. That would be Mr. Mengeles. Not to criticize you, dear, but the two of us have plans, and you didn't call ahead, now, did you?"

"Just a minute, Mother!" Roger cried, shrugging off her insistent hands on his shoulders. He dug his fingers into a box full of tissue paper, burrowing past baseball gloves and a pair of broken binoculars. There had to be a ring in here somewhere!

"Roger!" his mother cried in her most commanding voice. "You have to leave right now!"

Roger knew what would happen next. He grabbed a nearby shoebox to fend off his mother's hands when they grabbed his hair to drag him away.

The bell rang again, stopping his mother in mid-grab. The shoebox fell to the floor with a thump, followed by an odd little ping.

"I have to go up there right now!" His mother gave him one of her sternest looks, reserved for those occasions when you had done something slightly worse than blowing up the high school.

"If you are not right behind me when I open the front door," she yelled from halfway up the stairs, "you will be in trouble!"

Roger nodded his head as his mother disappeared upstairs. Why had the shoebox gone "ping"? He looked down at his feet. Actually, it hadn't been the shoebox, but a small wad of tissue paper that had fallen out and hit a pipe that led to the hot water heater. Heart in his throat, Roger tore the paper in two.

It was a Captain Crusader Decoder Ring.

Roger whispered a silent prayer to whatever god was in charge of putting free prizes in cereal boxes and ran up the stairs after his mother.

She opened the front door as he approached. "Oh, Mr. M!" she cried. "What a surprise!"

A balding gentleman sporting a pencil-thin mustache stood on the front steps. When he smiled, Roger saw he had a gold tooth.

"It was such a nice day, Mrs. G," the newcomer bubbled, "that I thought I might come for a visit."

"Oh, Mr. M!" Roger's mother gushed. "You're always so thoughtful! I'd like you to meet my son, Roger. You were just leaving, weren't you, Roger?"

Roger quickly stuffed the decoder ring in his pocket and shook the balding gentleman's hand. He had the oddest feeling that he had met this fellow before. Perhaps it was something about that pencil-thin mustache.

"Any son of Mrs. G," Mengeles was saying, "must be quite a son indeed!"

"Oh, yes," his mother interjected. "Roger is a sweet boy, if a trifle absent-minded. It really is a shame that he has to leave the house this very minute, isn't it, Roger?"

"Um," Roger replied as he let the gentle but firm pressure of his mother's hands push him past the older man. "Yes, Mother. Can't stay. Have to go. Awfully nice meeting you, sir—"

"Won't you come in, Mr. M?" His mother's voice cut through Roger's pleasantries as she ushered the older man through the door. "It was awfully nice to see you, dear," his mother called to Roger over Mr. Mengeles' shoulder. "Do plan to stay longer next time you're—"

His mother's voice was cut off by the slamming of the front door.

Roger shrugged. This had worked out to his advantage as well. He had been able to get in and out of his mother's house without having to provide a single explanation. Roger laughed out loud. He could almost kiss Mr. Mengeles' balding pate. But there was no time for that now. He had a decoder ring to decipher. Somewhere out there, in something called the "Cineverse," Delores was in danger.

Roger resisted an urge to throw the decoder ring across the room. Big Louie had said they were extremely breakable. Big Louie had also left without giving Roger the slightest clue as to how these rings worked.

Roger had returned to his apartment in good spirits, full of the best intentions. He had folded his bed back into a sofa, and drawn the blinds so he wouldn't be distracted. He sat back on the couch, determined to discover the ring's secret, and found himself becoming distracted anyway.

The problem wasn't that he didn't know how to work the Captain Crusader Decoder Ring. The problem was that he knew the decoder ring too well. The more he looked at the tiny gray dial the more secret messages returned from his childhood: "Always listen to what your teacher says." "Brush your teeth after every meal." "The policeman is your friend." How many messages just like that had he decoded so many years ago, perhaps with this very ring? They filled his head, making it difficult to concentrate on anything else, as if his thoughts had been taken over by some deranged social studies teacher.

How could this be the key to the universe?

Roger swallowed hard. Whatever his personal feelings, if he were to believe Delores—indeed, if he were to save Delores from whatever horrible fate awaited her—this cheap plastic ring was central to the problem.

If only he could get it to work!

He had to concentrate. Delores hadn't really even begun her demonstration when they were interrupted by Doctor Dread and his double-breasted minions. And he had been too upset to even watch Dread as the snakeskin-suited villain had spirited Delores away. The only time he had really seen the ring in use was in Big Louie's somewhat clumsy exit.

He had thought, initially, that he could simply reproduce the diminutive henchman's actions. First off, he was pretty sure Big Louie had turned the dial on his ring halfway around. He could only hope the ring had originally been set on "zero." If so, Roger could set his ring for the same destination.

But he had turned the ring every which way innumerable times. The only thing that happened were those civic messages constantly filling Roger's head. What had Big Louie done that Roger had forgotten?

Unless—

No, Roger thought, that was stupider than stupid. Then

again, what did he have to lose? He was alone in his own home, the curtains drawn against the outside world. He could say and do whatever he wanted to.

Roger twisted the ring again.

"See you in the funny papers," he whispered in a voice he hoped was as gruff as Big Louie's.

The room was filled with blue smoke.

Roger clasped the ring in his right hand. He was on his way.

CHAPTER

3

Roger coughed. Somehow, the blue smoke had turned to brown.

"Who's that?" a voice called out.

"I say we kill 'im!" another voice replied.

The first voice laughed gruffly. "Just hold your horses there, and wait for the dust to clear."

So it wasn't smoke after all. At least, not anymore. Now it was dust. Well, no matter what it was, it still made Roger cough. He could barely make out two figures through the brown haze.

Roger forgot all about his cough as the haze cleared.

"I say we kill 'im!" the second man repeated.

"Don't look familiar," the first man observed. "Think he's a Cavendish?"

Roger's throat felt much too dry. The two men staring at him looked disturbingly familiar. He recognized the boots, the spurs, the chaps, and the ten-gallon hats from a thousand B-Westerns. He recognized the rocks, sagebrush, cactus, and scraggly trees that now surrounded them from those same movies—the perfect place for an ambush or a chase on horseback. He wished he didn't recognize the shiny silver six-shooters each man had pointed at Roger's chest.

"Hey," said the first man, who wore a bright red bandanna over his embroidered yellow shirt. "You a Cavendish?"

"What?" Roger asked.

"Watch out!" warned the second man, who was dressed all in black except for an ornate silver belt buckle and a smaller, but no less ornate, band of silver around his hat. "Those Cavendish vermin are tricky!"

"What's a Cavendish?" Roger asked.

"See, what'd I tell you?" Black-and-Silver cried. "I say we kill 'im!" He smiled as he cocked his gun.

"Wait a second, Bart," Red-and-Yellow drawled easily. "You've gotta give him a chance to answer. That's one of the Laws of the West."

"You think the Cavendish pigs obey those laws?" Bart reluctantly eased the hammer down on his six-shooter. "But you're right. Otherwise we're no better than those Cavendish curs." He waved his gun in Roger's direction. "Okay, stranger. Thanks to Bret here, you got a minute to explain yourself before you start saying your prayers!"

Roger thought fast. What would you say to somebody in a Western who had a gun pointed at you?

"Uh—" he began. "I come in peace."

The two cowpokes frowned. Roger could see why—that didn't sound at all right. That was the sort of thing you said to Indians just before Geronimo or some two-faced white trader with a wagonload of guns and firewater showed up, and everybody ended up circling the wagons so they could be shot by the hero.

"Uh—" he tried again. "The name's Roger. I'm just driftin'. No particular place to go."

That went over a little better. The two cowboys looked a little more interested and a little less threatening. Roger hoped he was on the right track.

"No place to hang my hat that I'd call home," he added.

The cowboys frowned at that all over again.

"Of course," he added hurriedly, "I lost my hat."

Under the scrutiny of this pair from some all-too-distant cinematic past, Roger had become painfully aware of exactly what he was wearing. It was no wonder that these cowboys were suspicious. Before this, they'd probably never even seen a blue jogging outfit with white stripes down the side and matching running shoes. He wondered if there might be any way he could put their suspicions to rest. He hastily pulled out the pockets of his running pants.

"Look," he added. "I even lost my gun."

Bart turned to Bret. "Should we believe him?"

Bret squinted behind his revolver, as if he were taking better aim. This didn't seem to be working at all. Roger decided he'd better come up with another story, fast.

" 'Course," he added, "I never did tell you fellows about why I left home, and my dear little sweetheart, Emmy Lou—"

Bret shook his head. "I don't know. Something's wrong with him. Maybe he's a little slow in the head."

Both guns were now pointing straight for Roger's head. There had to be some way out of this! Roger cleared his throat. " 'Course," he added, "that was before I got jumped by Apaches—"

Bart and Bret glanced at each other as they simultaneously pulled back the hammers on their six-shooters.

"Uh—er," Roger added hurriedly. "Then there was that lynch mob who mistook me—"

Bart gently released the gun hammer as he spat in the dust. "He seems a little loony if you ask me." The man in black strode up to Roger, his spurs a'jangling. He poked his six-shooter at Roger's chin. "Mister, you came to the wrong town when you came to Sagebrush. We already got a town drunk."

Bret strode to his fellow cowboy's side to wave his gun at Roger's nose. "Yeah, and we're right proud of him, too. So don't get any ideas in that loony head of yours. We like Old Doc just the way he is." A smile cracked his weathered face. "Why, I can't think of anybody I'd rather see fishing quarters out of a spittoon."

"Yeah," Bart agreed. "Doc sure as heck does do a good grovel." He chuckled. "The way he crawls across the floor, lapping whiskey out of the sawdust—"

"And how about when he gets the shakes?" Bret twirled his six-gun merrily a few inches from Roger's forehead. "I'll tell you, when Doc needs whiskey, he does a mean square dance."

The two of them laughed together. "And how about his visions?" Bart poked his gun cheerfully into Roger's ribs. "Heck, he don't see no snakes or rats or spiders. Nobody sees visions as good as Doc. When he's comin' down off a drunk, he sees camels!"

"Yeah!" Bret chimed in. "And dromedaries!"

Bart frowned. "What's a dromedary?"

Bret frowned in turn. "Well, I'm not too sure myself. Doc's the one who saw it. I think it's some kind of special camel with extra humps. Either that, or some kind of pitted date." Bret shook his head in wonder. "That's our Doc. Imagine, having drunken visions of dried fruit."

"Whoo-ee!" Bart whistled. "All this talkin' about Doc has made me thirsty. I guess we're not going to kill you after all." He thrust his six-gun back in its holster. "You should be plumb grateful, stranger. The least you could do is buy us a drink."

He put a comradely hand around Roger's shoulder, gently but firmly turning Roger around, and began to guide him toward a distant group of buildings. As they approached what Roger realized must be the local town, he could hear the faint sounds of gunfire and the almost inaudible tinkling of a player piano.

"Yeah," Bret said, pushing Roger along from the other side. "You should buy us a couple at least. Out of sheer gratitude."

Roger let himself be eased into town by the two cowboys. What else could he do? He listened to two sets of spurs a'jangle as their owners led him towards what passed for civilization in this place. Their walk through the sagebrush gave him his first chance to think since he'd shown up here.

Why had the ring brought him to the Old West? Was this where he was supposed to end up? Somehow, this didn't seem to be the sort of place one would expect to find some-one like Big Louie. Maybe he could pull out the Captain Crusader Decoder Ring and try it again. But try for where? Only now—walking between two Tom Mix rejects toward a saloon where there was bound to be trouble (there was always trouble in B-Western saloons)—only now did Roger realize the true difficulty of his situation. It was one thing to be all noble and heroic when your beloved was in hideous danger. It was another thing to try and be all noble and heroic when the key to the universe looked suspi-ciously like a cheap and easily breakable plastic ring; a ring which, incidentally, he hadn't the slightest clue how to operate.

But he had more immediate problems than learning to use his decoder ring. His two trigger-happy companions expected Roger to buy them a drink. With what? Roger hadn't thought to stick his wallet in his jogging suit. Regu-lar old Earth-type money wouldn't be any good here any-way, would it? He did feel a flat piece of plastic in his jacket pocket, but still—unless B-Western saloons took Mastercard—Roger was in a lot of trouble.

Maybe, he thought, he could use the ring to get out of here. Of course, the next place he ended up might be even worse than this. Roger suppressed thoughts of suddenly appearing in a pit full of lions in some Roman epic, or perhaps materializing in the cockpit of a World War II fighter bomber just before it is hit by the enemy and bursts into flames. He'd have to examine the ring more carefully before he used it again.

Roger felt some added pressure at his back.

"Can't you move a little faster?" Bart snickered. "At the speed we're goin', we're all gonna die of thirst."

"Yeah," Bret added. "What kind of a town drunk are you if you can't even make it to the saloon?"

The cowboys laughed as if that was the funniest thing they had ever heard.

Roger clenched the Captain Crusader Decoder Ring

even more tightly in his hand. Whatever he did, he had to wait until he was alone. If someone got curious about that little plastic ring, and broke it or took it away at gunpoint, he would be stuck in Sagebrush for the rest of his life.

The three of them passed the blacksmith's shop, the first of half a dozen weathered buildings huddled together at the desert's edge. A bullet whizzed past Roger's ear.

Now that Roger thought of it, the rest of his life might not be all that long.

Two men appeared on opposite sides of the dusty street, one from behind a barber pole, the other from behind a rain barrel. Roger noticed with some distress that their guns were drawn.

"Whoa!" Bart called to the newcomers. "This fellow's with us."

"So he's not one of those Cavendish scum?" one of the other men called. They were both dressed more or less alike, in faded browns and blues, as if they wanted their clothes to blend in with the windswept desert and town. The two slowly approached Roger and his companions. They made no move to holster their guns.

"If he's a Cavendish, they've really lowered the entrance requirements." Bart pointed at Roger. "I mean, take a look at him."

Both newcomers paused to squint at Roger. They glanced at each other and holstered their weapons.

"That's more like it," Bart drawled. "Let me introduce you to the boys. I'd like you to meet Slim and Sam." Both Slim and Sam nodded in turn. Roger wasn't quite sure which one was which. "Slim, Sam—Roger here is gonna buy us all a drink."

"Really?" Slim (or it might have been Sam) slapped Roger's left shoulder. "Right neighborly of you."

"Yeah," Sam (or possibly Slim) chimed in as he jostled Roger's right side. "You should mention this sort of thing when you come into town. Saves a lot of shooting."

Roger found himself propelled by four pairs of hands through the swinging doors of the saloon.

The most disheveled man Roger had ever seen fell off a

chair in front of him. He groaned, turning his bloodshot eyes to stare at the new arrivals. He uttered a tremendous belch, then began to drag himself across the sawdust-strewn floor, heading straight toward Roger.

"A shtranger!" the incredibly filthy fellow called as he approached. "Hey, shtranger—how'sh about buying—a drink for a—guy who'sh down on hish—" The remainder of the man's sentence was lost in a coughing fit.

"This here is Doc," Bart remarked, nudging the rag-clad man crawling by his feet.

"Yeah." Bret chuckled. "Now you see what we mean. Is Doc a town drunk or is he a town drunk? How could you even hope to compete?"

Doc's hand shook as he reached for Roger's foot.

Roger had to admit this crawling, belching fellow was really into his role.

"Yeah," Bart mused. "It's hard to look at this disgusting shell of a man and think that once, not so many years ago, he was a great doctor."

"One of the best in the territory," Slim added. Unless it was Sam. Roger wasn't too sure.

Doc clawed weakly at Roger's sneaker. He made a retching sound deep in his throat.

"And he was one of the fastest guns around here, too," Bret added. "He was the best there was, northwest of the Pecos."

"Well, I don't know about that," Sam (or conceivably Slim) argued. "What about Dakota Jim Grady?"

Bret nodded solemnly. "Forget about Grady." He paused to reconsider. "Well, Doc was the fastest, west northwest of the Pecos."

This time the others nodded in agreement. Doc moaned by Roger's feet. The retching sound was a lot louder this time, as if it were guiding something upwards from deep inside Doc's throat. Roger carefully pulled his sneaker out of the way.

"'Course, you fellows forget," Sam (then again, it could have been Slim) remarked, "about what a mean violin player Doc was."

"Jush—down on my—luck." Doc pulled weakly at Roger's pant leg before he began to cough again.

"Yeah, and a crackerjack accountant too," Slim (still, it might be Sam) replied.

The four men again nodded solemnly. Doc seemed to have passed out on the floor.

Bart laughed whimsically. "Yeah, and how about the way he could juggle flaming hoops while making assorted bird calls of the American West?—but all this talking has made me thirsty." He kicked Doc's prostrate form out of the way. "Wasn't there somebody here that was going to buy us a drink?"

Roger found himself pushed to the bar. The old, one-eyed grizzled barkeep looked up from behind the far end of the polished wooden plank, where he busied himself polishing shot glasses with his apron.

"Four whiskeys," Bart demanded. He looked at the others. "Unless somebody besides me wants a drink, too?"

"Give us a bottle." Bret smiled. "And five glasses. We want Roger to join us, don't we, boys?"

"Wait a second." The bartender hobbled toward his new customers, his one good eye darting back and forth between Roger and the others. Roger noticed he had placed one hand on a shotgun he kept at the back of the bar. "Who's going to pay for these?"

Roger looked at his four drinking companions. They all smiled at him, their respective hands resting lightly on their respective gun handles. Well, this was it, then. He silently said a last farewell to Delores.

Bart frowned. "You do have money, don't you, Roger?"

"Hey," Bret said. "That's right. There wasn't nothing in his pockets!"

"You got something to pay for this, don't you?" Bart glanced meaningfully at the other cowboys. "Maybe I should have killed 'im after all." He grabbed Roger's wrist. "What are you holding so tightly in your hand?"

They were after his ring! Roger pulled away, punching the cowboy in the belly.

His actions only startled Roger for a second. After all,

death was one thing. His Captain Crusader Decoder Ring was something else again!

The four cowboys stared at Roger in disbelief.

"Wait a minute, fellows," Roger began, hoping against hope he might be able to talk his way out of this thing after all. "Even in lawless towns like this, you don't shoot unarmed men. That's one of the Laws of the West."

The four paused a long moment, considering, Roger was sure, just what laws they were ready to break.

There was a commotion on the street outside—gunshots, shouts, the sound of running feet.

"Mr. Bret! Mr. Bart!" A youngster came bursting through the swinging saloon doors. "Mr. Slim! Mr. Sam!"

Bart turned to the out-of-breath youth. "What is it, Jimmy?"

The boy could only manage one word:

"Cavendish!"

"So those maggots have finally come to town!" Bart smiled grimly. "Somebody get this Roger fellow a gun. It looks like he might have some backbone after all. And he's gonna need it against the Cavendishes!"

Bart and Bret and Slim and Sam (or possibly Sam and Slim) ran out into the street. Roger stared out after them, temporarily overcome by this sudden turn of events. How terrible were these Cavendishes, anyway?

The enormity of the situation hit Roger with one thought: Those fellows who were forcing him to buy them drinks were the good guys. According to Bart and the rest, the Cavendishes were much worse.

That's when the shooting began.

CHAPTER

4

Somebody handed Roger a six-shooter.

Startled, he looked up into the face of the old bartender.

"If you're gonna stand around here," the barkeep said as he plugged shells into his shotgun, "might as well help me defend the place. You get the front room. I'm going upstairs to see if I can get the drop on 'em."

The old man turned and limped up the stairs with amazing speed.

The gunfire outside sounded like it was getting closer. Roger looked down at the gun in his hand, worn silver with a mother-of-pearl handle. He didn't have the faintest idea how to use it. He quickly stuffed the Captain Crusader Decoder Ring in his jacket pocket, behind the Mastercard. If he could help it, he didn't want anything happening to his key to the Cineverse.

The bundle of rags stirred at his feet.

"Excushe me, shtranger." Doc rolled over and groaned.

A cowboy appeared at the door. It was either Sam or Slim. There were gunshots somewhere down the street. Either Sam or Slim turned and fired.

"You can appreciate—" Doc grunted, and somehow managed to get himself into a sitting position, "when a fella needsh a drink?"

The answering gunshots were much closer than before. Either Slim or Sam cried out and clutched at his shoulder. He raised his own pistol and fired again.

Roger didn't want to take his eyes off the door. "The bartender's gone," he said to Doc. "Imagine you can help yourself to all the whiskey you want."

Doc twisted his head around to look at the bar. "Land o'Goshen!" he exclaimed, timbre returning to his voice. "I've made it to heaven at lasht." He began to crawl through the sawdust in the general direction of the bar. "And all thish time I thought I wash shtuck in Sagebrush."

Yet another gun answered Sam's. Unless it was Slim's. Whoever he was, he crumpled onto the weathered walkway by the door.

Roger retreated to Doc's side. It looked like the Cavendishes were killing the good guys. Roger stared down at his gun. How did cowboys shoot other cowboys in old B-Westerns? You just pulled the trigger, didn't you?

A very large, mangy-looking fellow dressed all in black, without any of Bart's redeeming silver, filled the wide doorway to the saloon.

He smiled when he saw Roger. He had three teeth, maybe four if you counted a yellow stump. Roger fumbled with his pistol. Why were his hands sweating so much?

"Die, hombre!" the toothless fellow remarked.

Roger's heart was pounding in his ears. He pulled his gun up too fast. It flew out of his hand, skittering across the floor to land against Doc's posterior.

"Yeah." The toothless one raised the largest six-shooter Roger had ever seen. "I like to play with guns, too."

Roger heard two shots. He opened his eyes to see the large man fall like a mighty timber. The floor shook when he landed.

Roger turned to Doc, who held a smoking gun in his trembling hand.

"You shot him!"

"Of coursh I shot him." Doc waved the gun as if to shoo away any objections Roger might have. "Thish ish sher-ioush bishinessh! I mean, ther'sh nobody behind the bar. Took two shots, though." He resumed his crawl, aiming this time to get to the rear of the bar.

"I'll shoot better"—Doc wheezed—"onche I have a drink."

Numbly, Roger followed Doc to the bar. The old fellow had managed to prop himself up against the mirror on the back wall. Somewhat unsteadily, he grabbed a bottle and a pair of shot glasses, and maneuvered them very carefully until all three rested in front of Roger.

"Hate to drink alone," Doc explained. "Will you do the honorsh?"

Roger poured them each a shot. Doc drained his in a gulp and sighed in satisfaction.

"That'sh more like it," he intoned, his voice stronger than before. He studied the empty shot glass philosophi-cally. "It'sh not eashy being the town drunk, you know."

Roger nodded and took a sip from his glass. He started to cough as soon as the whiskey hit the back of his throat. It felt like his tonsils were on fire!

"Yesh," Doc agreed. "Good shtuff, ishn't it? When you're the town drunk, you don't often get the good shtuff. It'sh a real reshponshibility, let me tell you. You have to be good at crawling acrossh the floor, for one thing. And vi-shions! They alwaysh exshpect you to have vishions!"

Doc pushed his shot glass toward the half-full bottle. Roger poured him another.

"I shee camelsh, you know," Doc admitted.

Sam (or possibly Slim) coughed where he lay by the doorway to the saloon. So he was still alive! Maybe there was something Roger and Doc could do to help him.

But wait! Someone was coming! Roger could hear gruff voices and a number of spurs a'jangling.

"I can't help it if I shee camelsh." Doc drained his glass again. "Or wash it dromedariesh?"

The gun! What had happened to the gun? Roger looked

frantically around the sawdust-strewn floor, but he couldn't see it anywhere. Did Doc still have it?

"Humpsh! Thatsh—what it wash." This time, Doc refilled the shot glass himself. "Humpsh have always been my undoing." Doc paused to drain the glass again. "Or maybe it wash mumpsh."

Three men burst into the saloon. All were dressed in black. All smiled toothless smiles.

"Die, hombres!" they cried together.

Doc casually shot them.

"Now, where wash I?" Doc stared blearily at his shot glass. "Oh, yesh. Camelsh!"

"You shot all of them!" Roger exclaimed.

Doc nodded. "Told you I'd be better onche I had a drink. Shteady's the hand, you know. Great medical value." Doc poured himself another.

They heard the sound of other running feet. Doc slowly swung his six-shooter back toward the door.

He let the gun fall when he saw it was Bart and Bret. The two cowboys stared at their prone friend.

"They shot Slim!" Bret exclaimed.

"Slim?" Bart remarked. "I always thought this one was Sam!"

Whichever one it was groaned again.

"He's still alive!" Bart called.

"He need's doctorin'," Bret agreed. "But who can—?" He left the question unfinished.

Doc wearily pushed himself away from the back of the bar. "I'll do it!" He walked steadily to the swinging doors. "You boys get Sam or Slim here into the back room, I'll do the rest." As an afterthought, he added. "Anybody here got a pocketknife?"

Bart fished in his pocket and handed Doc his. The two cowboys picked up their wounded comrade and carried him past Roger, through a doorway to the left of the bar.

When Bart and Bret walked back into the saloon, they noticed the bodies.

Bart whistled. "Roger doesn't just have a mean right hook. He can shoot, too."

Roger started to object, but Bret had already picked up the bottle and was pouring the three of them a round.

"As long as the barkeep is upstairs," Bret drawled, "I think it's time for us to buy Roger a drink."

Roger heard a rapid hobbling sound coming down the stairs. He turned to see a grim-faced bartender descending towards them.

"Just a darn tootin' minute!" the aged barkeep cried. "Who's going to pay for all this?"

Bart smiled up at the old man. "How about the Cavendishes?"

Instead of answering, the bartender glared back up the stairs. There, Roger saw, on the very top stair, were a pair of snow-white boots.

The owner of the boots slowly began to walk down, a step at a time. Roger saw that the man had pure white chaps, and pure white jeans, and a shining white horse-head-shaped enamel belt buckle for his white leather belt.

The bartender scurried down the stairs to get out of the newcomer's way.

The white-booted man took another step, then another. Roger saw that his shirt was covered with white fringe, and he wore a white bolo tie.

The stranger continued his descent. The straight line of his jaw looked oddly familiar, but Roger imagined he had seen the same noble jaw line on a hundred Western heroes. He was cleanshaven, with a firm mouth and a long aquiline nose. But the top half of his face was covered by a white mask tied behind his head so that it covered most of his blond hair as well, with only two small holes cut for the eyes.

The stranger placed two immaculately manicured fingers on his pure white Stetson, and tipped it ever so slightly at the group standing before the bar.

"Heard there might be a little trouble," the stranger's deep bass voice mentioned.

"Oh, no, Mr. Marshal," Bret hurriedly explained. "No trouble here at all."

"Shucks, Mr. Marshal," Bart chimed in. "We were only having a little harmless fun."

"Perhaps," the marshal mused thoughtfully. "Why don't you fellows pay up for your drinks?"

Bart and Bret quickly dug into their pockets.

Casually, as if it might be an afterthought, the marshal remarked: "I hear there might be some Cavendishes in town."

Bart nodded rapidly. "Yep! The whole bunch!"

"Well, that bunch isn't as thick as it used to be." He glanced at the bodies littered about the room. "I see a few members spread out on the floor." He patted his white-handled pistol in its pure white holster. A slight smile played across his lips. "And Betsy here got one or two as well."

He looked around the room. "I think you fellows can clean up here. Now, if you'll excuse me, I've got some Cavendishes to collect."

He turned back to them as he reached the swinging door. "Be careful," he said as he tipped his hat a final time. "Remember: Civic responsibility is everybody's business!"

And with that, he was gone.

Roger felt a sudden chill run down his spine. There was something about that fellow—something oddly familiar.

"Who was that man?" he asked.

"Why, didn't you know?" the old barkeep asked in wonder. "That's the Masked Marshal!"

"Hey!" Bart called. "Listen!"

"Yeah!" Bret agreed. "Doc must have fixed Slim up."

"Yeah!" Bart echoed. "Or maybe it was Sam."

From somewhere in the back of the building, Roger could hear the faint strains of a violin.

"Freeze, hombres!" came a deep voice from the door.

Roger spun to look. The doorway was full of Cavendishes!

Yet another large man in black—one of a number of them crowding the door—grinned a toothless smile. "It took forever for that Masked Marshal to leave. Now that he's gone, though, we can take over this place!"

Cavendishes started to file into the room. A lot of Cavendishes.

"I'd like to introduce you to a few of my boys." The lead Cavendish leered toothlessly. "It's the least we can do for you hombres, before we plant you up on Boot Hill."

He pointed to the men in black farthest from him. "These here are Tex and Dakota. You boys check upstairs, then keep watch out some windows to make sure the marshal doesn't come back."

Tex and Dakota quickly climbed the stairs. The speaking Cavendish spat a wad of tobacco juice at the corner spittoon. Despite himself, Roger wondered how the fellow could chew anything with so few teeth.

"The next two are Arizona and Kansas," the lead Cavendish further drawled. "You fellas get in that back room, and see who's playing that violin!"

Arizona and Kansas did as they were ordered.

The lead Cavendish nodded toward another pair. "California and Colorado here are going to keep an eye on a few of you until Boss Cavendish comes. What's this, though?" He pointed at Roger. "I see a new face."

He walked halfway across the saloon in three very long steps. A hand the size of most people's heads grabbed Roger's running jacket and pulled the smaller man toward him. "You're dressed almost as strange as the Masked Marshal. You wouldn't happen to be his sidekick?"

Roger rapidly shook his head.

The big man laughed. "You wouldn't tell me if you were. Sidekicks are that way, noble and self-sacrificing. It's one of the Laws of the West." He shook his head. "I'm afraid, my sidekick friend, that you might be too much trouble for us. We might just have to put you out of the way before Boss Cavendish shows." He turned and pointed at one of the black-garbed men hanging slightly behind all the rest.

"Idaho!"

A man much shorter than all those around him replied: "Yeah, boss?"

The big man pointed to Roger and smiled. "Take this sidekick out and shoot him!"

The small man stepped forward. The gun quivered in his hand. Wait a moment! It took Roger a minute to recognize this fellow, now that he was wearing a black-fringed shirt and ten-gallon hat. But he was sure of it—he'd recognize that trembling gun and wishy-washy manner anywhere.

"You better move, you two-bit—um, I mean—you big galoot!" the small man managed. His gun was really shaking now.

Roger couldn't believe his eyes! It was Big Louie!

"Out of my way, lackey!" a voice shouted from outside.

"Uh-oh," the leader said. "That's the Boss. Looks like you get to live for a few more minutes, sidekick. 'Course, Boss Cavendish knows a lot more interesting ways to die than a simple bullet through the heart." The big man smiled so broadly this time that Roger could actually see a few rotting, discolored molars set deep in the gums.

"Good, good," Boss Cavendish's all-too-familiar voice chortled outside. "You've done just what I asked." The voice laughed. "Now there are things to be—dealt with. Now there are things to be—taken care of."

A tall, thin man stood in the door, framed by late afternoon sunlight. The black snakeskin coat didn't fool Roger for one second. The man who stood in the doorway—the man they called Boss Cavendish—was really Doctor Dread!

CHAPTER

5

Doctor Dread frowned.

"What is this?"

"We think he's a sidekick, Boss," one of the hulking black-clad fellows fawned. "Maybe even the Masked Marshal's sidekick!"

Dread grunted. "A sidekick? Well, he's certainly dressed—strangely enough." His frown vanished as he talked, the evildoer warming to his topic. "However, I am privileged to have—other information. I know—heh—certain things about this—hehheh—stranger, things that should have been reported in the—hehhehheh—past tense, if you get my drift."

"Oh, yeah, Boss!" A half-dozen Cavendishes pointed their six-shooters at Roger's head. "Past tense!"

Everybody in the gang except Big Louie laughed heartily. Big Louie tried to step back, but the Cavendishes were ranked too closely behind him. The small fellow stopped abruptly, almost tripping over his spurs.

Doctor Dread turned his slightly maniacal gaze at the

diminutive gunfighter. The fringe on the Boss's black
leather glove shook as he pointed at Louie.

"But you're—not laughing," Dread purred.

"Pardon me, Doctor—I mean, Boss Cavendish," Big
Louie blurted. "It was an oversight. I enjoy a joke as much
as the next—uh—cowboy. Ha-ha, sir."

But Dread/Cavendish refused the apology with a curt
shake of his head. "No, it's—too late now." He glanced
back at Roger, the sardonic smile once again playing at his
lips. "In fact, it's—hehhehheh—too late for both of you!"

His black-gloved hand whipped around to grab Big
Louie's bright red bandanna. "We have to have a—little
talk, Big—" Dread coughed apologetically. "I beg your
pardon. What's your name—hehheh—around here?"

"I-Idaho," Louie quivered.

"Figures," Boss Cavendish/Doctor Dread replied dryly.
He pointed at Roger with his free glove. "Idaho, why
hasn't this man been"—he paused meaningfully—"removed?"

"Uh—" Big Louie/Idaho stalled. "You mean—um—
why hasn't he been—uh—dealt with?"

"No, I mean why hasn't he been"—he hesitated—"sent
away on a permanent vacation! What do you think I mean?
Haven't I made myself clear, time after time? And yet—
hehhehheh"—he tugged purposefully on Louie's bandanna
—"you've—hehheh—let me down."

"But, Boss—" Idaho pleaded, trying to think fast and
failing utterly. "He had a gun. Well, no, actually he didn't
have a gun, but he didn't have a ring. That is, I didn't
think he had a ring, so I didn't want to waste my gun. I
mean, my bullets."

Idaho looked around to the other bad guys for some sort
of help. Unfortunately for him, at that precise moment all
the other bad guys seemed far too involved in studying the
intricacies of their individual six-shooters, or the dust on
their boots, or the tobacco in their mouths, or anything else
beside Idaho.

"You know, bullets!" the short gunslinger went on anyway. "Uh—lefty only gave me five, and I had no idea

when I could get any more, still being in my probationary period as a bad guy and all, so I thought, my boss will be proud of me if I *save* my bullets for something really worthwhile, say bank-robbing or posse-shooting—"

"Boys," Dread said to the others as he completely ignored Louie's groveling. "I have a—hehhehheh—job for you."

All the other black-clad cowboys laughed even louder than before. Half a dozen thumbs clicked back the hammers of their six-shooters.

"Now, boys," Dread chided. "You misunderstand me. Let's not be overeager. I don't want—hehheh—anything done around here. I think it would be better if we took our friends here on a—teeheehee—little walk. Say behind the"—snickersnicker—"feed store?"

From the way the cowboys laughed, Roger could tell they all thought it was an excellent idea. Dread turned to glare at him, his smile even more demented than before.

"But why does our intruder look so glum? I assure you, stranger, what happens next will be very"—he hesitated compellingly—"educational. You're going to have a chance to see a whole array of authentic Western weapons —hehhehheh—real close!"

One of the largest of the Cavendishes waved his gun at Roger's nose. "C'mon, hombres, it's time to get a'movin'. You've got a"—chuckle—"appointment on Boot Hill."

Roger sighed and let himself be led, side by side with Big Louie, out of the saloon. All six of the Cavendishes who had drawn their hardware came with them, forming a semicircle around the luckless duo once all of them had gotten through the saloon's swinging doors and out onto the dusty street.

Roger thought, for the merest instant, of making a run for it. After all, it was only fifty feet or so to the nearest cover. With six loaded guns aimed by six crack Western marksmen all pointed at him, why, they wouldn't have a chance to get off more than—say—twenty or thirty shots before he reached safety.

This was it, then. His search for Delores would end

with him in an unmarked grave, his corpse weighted down with Cavendish bullets. And, with his future, who knew what horrible fate awaited his beloved? Some kind of hero he was!

"Some kind of hero we both are!" Big Louie whispered. "I did try to keep you out of this. If you would have just had the sense to stay back on Earth, tied up in your blanket—" The henchman-turned-cowboy left the rest of the sentence unsaid as he scuffed his boots dejectedly in the dry Western soil.

"Yeah," Roger replied, glancing at his hangdog companion. He was surprised how sorry he could feel for someone who had previously threatened him with a loaded gun. But Big Louie was such a—Roger paused, trying to think of the right word—such a character! Yeah, that was it. That was it exactly.

Their black-clad companions continued to laugh among themselves. The largest of them, a full six foot six from his mud-caked boots to his ten-gallon hat, once again led the conversation.

"Well, boys, how are we going to do it?"

The other cowboys looked surprised.

"You mean—the job?" one asked hesitantly.

"That's right." The tall cowboy smiled. "And Boss Cavendish would expect us to do it with some style."

"I guess I'm going to get both of us killed," Roger admitted to Louie in a whisper. "I never thought about that when I followed you here."

Big Louie shrugged. "That's all right. If it hadn't have been you, it would have been somebody else. I realize now that I'm not cut out for bad-guying." He sighed, playing absently with the mother-of-pearl buttons on his cowboy shirt. "I should have stayed in comedy relief, where I belonged."

Roger had never seen anyone look so defeated. Maybe there was some way he could cheer the fellow up in their last moments together.

"Style?" one of the cowboys asked the others. "I

thought we were going to shoot them, you know, behind the feed store."

"Shooting?" the big gunfighter rumbled. "Behind the feed store? Where's the drama there?—those heart-tugging moments when we see these innocents unable to escape certain death? What kind of reputation are we Cavendishes going to get if we lower ourselves to shootings behind the feed store?"

The other cowboys grunted in agreement. One mumbled something about never thinking of it that way before.

Roger decided to ignore the discussion of their deaths for the time being. He nudged Big Louie.

"Actually, I didn't think you did so bad."

"Really?" Big Louie replied halfheartedly.

"Yeah," Roger agreed. "Especially when you showed up in my apartment. I didn't doubt for a minute that you were a gangster."

"You think so?" Louie looked up and squared his shoulders. "I was that tough, huh?"

"Absolutely," Roger replied, trying to be as truthful as possible. "I had never seen anything quite like you before."

"We could hang them!" one of the other cowboys suggested.

"Gee," Big Louie considered. "But I wasn't very good as a cowboy, was I?"

"Well—" Roger began, trying to think of something, anything, positive he might say.

"Now there's an idea!" the big fellow enthused. "Two innocents dangling in midair, their lives slowly choked away by a hangman's noose. That's a Cavendish idea, that's for plumb sure! Anybody know of any big trees around here?"

"It was that name, Idaho, wasn't it?" Big Louie continued before Roger could think of anything clever. "Yeah, I know it's not as good a name as Big Louie, but it was the only name they had left." He paused, glancing for an instant at his ornately tooled boots. "Well, that's not completely true. I did have some choice—they really had two names left. It was either Idaho, or the District of Columbia."

"Doesn't sound like much choice to me," Roger agreed. "I see what you mean."

"Anybody know of any smaller trees?" the large cowpoke asked after no one answered his earlier question. "Don't have to be much more than seven, eight feet."

"Yeah," Big Louie went on. "No other names left. The Cavendishes are a *big* gang!"

"Anybody know of any large bushes?" the leader asked at last. "Maybe we can think of some way to hang them sideways—or something."

"Sorry, Dakota," one of the other cowboys replied. "It's a desert town. Not a tree for miles."

"You're right, Kansas," the big gunfighter, Dakota, replied reluctantly. "But it was such a crackerjack idea!"

"There's always our guns," another suggested, "and the feed store."

"Guns?" Dakota moaned. "Feed stores? So the Cavendishes have to sink that low!"

"Wait a second," Kansas suggested. "What about a—cattle stampede?"

Dakota slapped Kansas on the back. "Now that's Cavendish thinking! The two of them with nowhere to run, confronted by a wall of marauding beasts whose only thought is fear! No matter where they go, no matter what they do, there is no escape! Then, in a moment of poignant terror, the mass of cattle overwhelm them, a thousand hooves pummeling their bodies beyond recognition!" The large cowboy sighed with satisfaction.

"It really is nasty, isn't it?" Kansas agreed.

"It's more than that!" Dakota chortled. "It's Cavendish nasty!"

"Uh, fellas?" interjected a third cowboy, the same one who had remarked that there weren't any trees. "There is one small problem."

"Not again!" Dakota groaned. "What is it this time, Nevada?"

"Well, correct me if I'm wrong," Nevada continued

haltingly, "but I don't think we have any cattle."

"No cattle?" Kansas blurted incredulously.

"Are you sure?" Dakota demanded. "None at all?"

"Well, you know," Nevada continued apologetically, "this being a desert town—"

"Wait a moment!" Kansas broke in. "Don't the Widow Johnson—"

"Why, that's right!" Nevada replied, hitting his chaps with a resounding slap. "The Widow Johnson's got cattle!"

"See?" Dakota chortled proudly. "If you're a Cavendish, you just got to be resourceful. Now, all we have to do is go over to the Widow's—"

"Uh—" Nevada cowered a bit as he spoke again. "There's still a slight problem."

"Problem?" Dakota frowned. "You mean the Widow Johnson doesn't have cattle after all?" He turned his gun ever so slightly, so that its muzzle was pointing a bit more toward Nevada than toward Roger and Louie. Roger thought again about making a break for it. With only five guns pointed at him, he'd probably only take fifteen to twenty rounds before he made it to safety.

"I would be very unhappy," Dakota drawled, "if, after all this time, the Widow Johnson didn't have cattle."

"I didn't say that!" Nevada replied abruptly. "She has cattle all right!"

"Well, why didn't you say so?" Dakota smiled easily as he once again aimed his gun at Roger's head. "You got me worried there for a minute."

"Uh—she just doesn't have very many cattle," Nevada added softly.

"How many does she have?" Kansas asked before Dakota could get annoyed again.

"Uh—two," Nevada answered.

"Two?" Dakota demanded.

"Well, yeah," Nevada replied defensively. "She's got to get her milk from somewhere."

"Two cows?" Dakota despaired. "How are we going to stampede somebody with two cows?"

"Well," Kansas suggested, "maybe we could have the

two of them stampede over these fellows a number of times. You know, after ten or fifteen runs back and forth—"

"No," Dakota said with finality. "Too messy. That ain't a Cavendish death." He waved at Nevada with his gun. "You're sure there're only two?"

"Well, you know," Nevada said as he took a step away, "this is a desert town—"

"Well, I suppose I can't shoot you for that." Dakota sighed. "But how are we going to kill them?"

"There's always our guns," someone piped up in the back. "And the feed store."

Dakota's six-shooter once again pointed at the speaker. "I don't want to hear that suggestion made again. Understand, Arkansas?"

Arkansas nodded vehemently.

"Good." Dakota's gun returned to guarding Roger. "Now come up with a Cavendish way of dealing with these scum!"

"Uh, uh—" Arkansas began. "Uh, we could—uh—throw them over a waterfall!"

"Throw them over a waterfall?" Dakota began derisively, but stopped himself. "Wait a darn tootin' minute. That idea ain't half bad. I can see them struggling uselessly against the current, their muscles giving out as they are pulled ever closer to the edge, their screams lost in the thunderous sound of cascading water as they are tossed like rag dolls onto the rocks below, their broken, bloody bodies on those granite slabs mute testimony to what happens when you cross the Cavendishes!" He laughed heartily. "Yeah, that ain't bad at all!"

"Uh—" Nevada interjected, even more hesitantly than before. "Dakota—"

"What?" the big cowpoke snapped. "The waterfall's a fine idea! What's your problem now?"

"Uh—" Nevada quavered. "This is a desert town—"

"Oh," Dakota remarked, stopping for a moment to stare at his gun. "Yeah." He glowered at the others. "Well, what's everybody waiting for? Let's get to the feed store. You heard Boss Cavendish!"

Roger felt himself being pushed to the right, straight for an alleyway between another saloon (so far, Roger had counted six) and a two-story building with a large red and yellow sign that proclaimed "Aldridge Feeds."

"You know, Dakota," Kansas drawled as the gang pushed into the alleyway behind Roger and Louie. "You can look on the bright side of all this. Sure, we have to shoot these guys, and behind the feed store, too. But that doesn't mean we have to bury them! Why not leave 'em lying there instead, two corpses exposed to the elements so that the buzzards can pick their bones, and there'll be nothing left but a pair of broken skeletons, bled white by the desert sun?"

"Hey, Kansas!" Arkansas cheered. "Now that sounds like a Cavendish job!"

"Oh, stop trying to cheer me up," Dakota grumbled sourly. "By now, I just want to get this over with. We'll stop them in back of the place, and then—"

A dark-garbed stranger stepped from behind the store to block their path. Roger and Louie stopped halfway down the alley, the six Cavendishes close behind them.

"I'd stop right there," the stranger said, "if I were you."

CHAPTER

6

The Cavendish gang stopped. So did Roger and Big Louie. The stranger smiled.

Roger thought there was something familiar about that smile. He'd seen it before somewhere. For an instant, he thought the stranger might be the Masked Marshal in disguise. But he wasn't tall enough, for one thing, and Roger doubted if, even in disguise, a pristine figure like the white-suited marshal would ever allow himself to look so disheveled.

"Now you boys are going to have to let your two guests go," the stranger drawled, "or there's gonna be a little shootin'."

"Oh, yeah?" Arkansas replied.

Before he could get his gun half-drawn, the stranger had shot him.

Arkansas clutched at his stomach, staggering forward three paces, then back two. He stared at the stranger as he slipped to his knees, then collapsed, face first, in a cloud of dust.

"Not bad," the stranger commented. "At least you Cavendishes know how to die right proper. So who's next? Any of the rest of you lookin' for a little extra ventilation?"

None of the remaining Cavendishes moved.

"Good." The stranger smiled, rubbing with his free hand at his unshaved chin. "Excuse me for a second." He reached in his pocket, fishing around for something. "Don't try anything!" He pulled out a flask and deftly unstoppered it with his thumb. "I shoot faster than I drink!"

It was only when the stranger lifted the flask to his lips that Roger realized who it was.

"That'sh better," Doc mumbled as he repocketed the flask. He hiccuped softly. "Pardon." He shook his head and blinked, as if trying to clear his head. "Sorry it took me so long to get around to rescuin' you fellas, but I had to do a little doctorin' first. Slim was in a bad way. Unless that was Sam I tended to."

"It's Doc!" Dakota exclaimed as he, too, recognized the disheveled figure. "I would have realized it sooner, but this is the first time I've ever seen him standing up. Wanna fish for pennies, Doc? There must be a spittoon around here somewhere."

The Cavendishes all laughed.

"Hey," Doc replied sourly as he once again retrieved his flask. "I'll thank you to keep a civil tongue in your head. I'm the one who's got the gun."

Dakota chortled. "That's right, boys. See who's got the drop on us? Why, it's the town drunk!"

"But, Dakota!" Kansas interjected. "The town drunk already shot Arkansas!"

"A lucky shot!" Dakota sneered. "Let's see how one gun stands up against five!"

"Duck!" Big Louie shouted. Roger followed the other man's lead as both of them dove into the dirt.

Doc shot the remaining Cavendishes before any of them had a chance to aim. All five staggered back and forth for a moment, clutching various parts of their anatomies, before they collapsed into a large Cavendish pile that filled the alleyway.

"Five more lucky shots," Doc announced. "I think that calls for a drink!"

He uncapped his flask and took four long swallows.

"Yeah!" Doc cheered when he finally took a breath. "That'sh more like it!" And he too fell, face first, into the dirt.

"Oh, dear," Roger remarked as he regained his feet, rather surprised by this turn of events. As he brushed the dust from his jogging suit, he peered down the alley at the prostrate Doc. "Is he drunk again?"

Big Louie whistled as he stood beside him. "Either that, or he really needed to take a nap."

Roger shook his head. "Well, at least he was nice enough to save us from certain death before he passed out."

Louie scowled, looking back the way they had come. "Well, at least he has for the moment. Doc may have gotten rid of our immediate problem, but the Cavendishes are a *big* gang!"

Before Roger could ask what Louie meant, he heard the commotion, a combination of angry shouts and running boots, complete with spurs a'jangling.

"Cavendishes!" Louie replied to Roger's horrified expression. "At least a dozen of them!"

"What are we going to do?" Roger whispered.

"Well, we do have a couple guns here." Louie knelt, picking up a pair of six-shooters dropped by recently deceased Cavendishes. "We could stand our ground in the alleyway, and face those dozen Cavendishes as they come around the corner. It would be the noble, dramatic thing to do."

He frowned as he curled his index finger around the trigger of the revolver in his right hand. "We can't pay much attention to the fact that I've never fired this type of gun before." He handed Roger the other revolver. "I would guess that you're not too experienced at this either. And, of course, we should pay no heed that there'll be a dozen to our two, and that all of them are seasoned gunfighters who know no mercy."

The crowd noise was getting closer. Roger thought it sounded angrier as well.

Big Louie's frown turned from his gun to his new-found companion. "On the other hand, we could hide."

"I've always wanted to see the inside of a feed store," Roger admitted. "But what should we do with Doc?"

"Drag him inside, I guess." Big Louie started toward their fallen savior at the alley's end. "Come on. That mob's going to be here in a second."

Roger ran to join Big Louie. He saw a weathered door in the back corner of the equally weathered feed store building. Maybe, he thought, they could drag Doc in there. Doc's eyes opened as they approached.

"Wait a shecond!" Doc demanded. "Keep your handsh off me!"

"But, Doc!" Roger began. "The Cavendishes!"

"Sho tha'sh what you are!" Doc's hand gripped his revolver. "Well, I've shot a few Cavendishesh in my time!"

"But—" Roger began again. He stopped abruptly when a bullet whizzed past his ear.

"Time for the feed store!" Big Louie proclaimed, already sprinting away toward the back door.

"But—" Roger looked one final time at Doc. The fallen man's gun swung back and forth as he attempted to aim. Roger quickly followed Louie. A pair of gunshots followed them.

Roger jumped inside the feed store, flattening himself against a rough-hewn wall. Louie slammed the door and bolted it shut. There was a faded poster tacked to the door's inside, advertising hog chow.

"You all right?" the small fellow managed after he'd regained his breath.

They were in a dimly lit storeroom. Roger nodded, looking about at the dusty shelves and hog- and chicken-chow posters as if they might give him some kind of answer.

"But—" he said haltingly. "I don't understand—"

"You mean Doc not recognizing us?" Louie chuckled.

"Well, his memory's not so good. Comes from all that drinking."

"No." Roger frowned. "No, that's not it."

"His eyesight's not that hot either. Mistaking us for Cavendishes!" Louie whistled. "And did you get a whiff of his breath?"

Mistaking them for Cavendishes? Roger decided not to remind Big Louie who else was dressed in official bad-guy black around here. Instead, he doggedly pursued his original question.

"No. What I wanted to know is, didn't Doc already shoot six Cavendishes?"

"Yep." From the way Louie laughed, Roger had uttered a real knee slapper. "You saw it too. What a shot!"

Roger realized he was going to have to be a little more obvious. "And doesn't he have a *six*-shooter?"

"Yep. A Colt Peacemaker. Standard gun of the West."

Roger sighed. Maybe he was missing something. He'd have to pursue these questions to the end. "And wouldn't you agree with me that he was far too drunk to reload?"

"Doc was far too drunk to be conscious!" Louie chortled.

This was it, then. Roger asked the final, logical question: "Well, then, how did he have any bullets left to shoot at us?"

Big Louie looked at him in surprise, then started laughing all over again. "Oh, that's easy. Haven't you ever heard of Movie Magic?"

"Um—" Roger replied hesitantly. "I guess so. Everybody's heard of Movie Magic." It was the sort of phrase that always popped up in documentaries about the Golden Age of Hollywood. He didn't add that, until this moment, he hadn't thought it really meant anything in particular.

"Well, that's what we're talking about here. We're in the Cineverse, you know!"

"Oh," Roger replied, still not really understanding at all. Delores had told him something of the Cineverse. But, as he recalled, they had been interrupted before her explanation had begun to make any real sense.

"You see," Big Louie continued, "you're trying to apply mathematical logic to this situation. That's the way things probably work back where you come from."

Roger guessed so. At least, that's the way they were supposed to work. He nodded.

"Well, they sure don't work that way around here. Like I said—Movie Magic. Look—Doc's a hero. Well, at least in this case he was, and, in the Cineverse, mathematics and logic don't apply to heroes."

"Don't apply?" Roger parroted. "So he can get more than six shots from a six-shooter?"

"No problem at all," Louie assured him. "Heroes can get twelve, eighteen, twenty-two shots off without reloading, and nobody thinks twice. It's a part of that Movie Magic. Good guys shooting bullets move the story along, so the bullets are there."

"So *that's* Movie Magic?" Roger mused, beginning to understand.

"What you can't begin to understand," Louie continued, "is that Movie Magic is different on every world in the Cineverse. In a place like this, it's pretty straightforward, rules like that gun thing, or the fact that should you pull your wagons in a circle, all the Indians in the vicinity are required to ride their horses around said circle in a clockwise direction, until all said Indians are shot."

"Really?" Roger replied, intrigued despite himself. "I always wondered about that."

"Oh, sure. You think any self-respecting Indian would do something as foolish as that otherwise? Of course, on a Western world like this, it's all pretty straightforward. Movie Magic gets a lot more complicated on other worlds. Witch doctors, magicians, vampires, mystics, sea serpents, all kinds of fantastic people and things, and all exercising their own brands of Movie Magic. If you ever land on one of their worlds, things can get sticky. But that's not the worst. If you ever get stuck on one of the musical worlds, forget it!"

Roger was about to ask exactly what it was he should forget, when he heard the Cavendishes.

"Hey!" a gruff voice cried outside their hiding place. "They got Dakota!"

"And Kansas!" another yelled.

"And Arkansas!" a third chimed in.

"They got all of them!" the first voice added. "Maybe Boss Cavendish—underestimated them?"

"Those guys?" another of the voices replied in disbelief. "But they both looked like *sidekicks*. Everybody knows sidekicks can't shoot!"

"You're right," the first voice replied. "There has to be some other explanation." He paused, then added in surprise: "Hey! Who's this?"

"Wha—Oh, that's just Doc, the town drunk."

"They've found Doc!" Roger whispered. "We've got to do something!"

"Just hold your horses, there!" Louie replied. "You like that? It's one of the Western phrases I managed to pick up. And me here only a matter of hours—"

"But Doc saved our lives—" Roger interjected.

"And tried to take them again, shortly thereafter," Louie reminded him. "Besides, what could we do? If we go rushing out there, the Cavendishes are probably going to expect us to do something with our guns."

"Something with our guns?" Roger replied, unable to keep the dread out of his voice. He had to admit that Big Louie could be persuasive when he wanted to be.

"Maybe that's our answer!" one of the Cavendishes yelled outside. "Maybe Doc helped them."

"The town drunk? Let's stop clownin' around. No, my guess is that someone else did some fancy shootin', and my second guess is that they're still around here someplace. Texas, check over there. Oregon, look back out on the street."

"They're going to find us!" Roger whispered, the panic rising in his voice.

"Not necessarily," Louie replied. "These are the bad guys. And bad guys, by the rules, can be pretty stupid."

"Movie Magic again?"

"You're catching on."

Roger was more than catching on. He had an idea. "But maybe that's our salvation. By the laws of Movie Magic, if those are the bad guys, and they're looking to kill us, doesn't that make us the good guys?"

Big Louie frowned. "Well, probably. By default, if nothing else."

"Then maybe we can shoot it out. If we're the good guys, we just have to wait for them to run out of bullets."

But Louie wasn't convinced. "It's not that simple. We may be good guys, but we may still just be sidekicks, too. And sometimes sidekicks get killed."

"Killed?" Roger replied with some disappointment.

"Yeah, it's called pathos. It helps move the plot along."

Roger sighed. "And anything that moves the plot along is Movie Magic?"

Louie nodded in approval. "You're learning fast. Besides, you can never tell when the bad guys will run out of bullets. That is, until it happens."

Roger shook his head. These rules seemed to get more complicated by the moment. "You mean—"

"Yeah, sometimes bad guys get more than six, too. But they do always run out of bullets before the good guys. 'Course, that doesn't always happen when they're shooting at sidekicks." Louie paused to look between the slats of the back door. "And there *are* twelve of them out there. That'll give some of them a chance to reload."

Sunlight streamed through a knothole a couple feet above the corner where Roger crouched. Boots clumped heavily back and forth outside, a' jangling spurs muted in the dirt. Roger resisted the urge to follow Louie's lead and peek out at the gang. If they were any match for their voices, they were twice as big and twice as ugly as the last group of Cavendishes.

"So there's no way to get out of here?" he asked despairingly.

"Didn't say that. This being the Cineverse, there's a certain order to everything. Maybe we *can* get them to use up all their bullets. Then, of course, they have to throw their guns."

"They have to?"

Big Louie nodded solemnly. "It's a compulsion. You get an empty gun, you have to throw it at the hero. You don't have to hit him, of course, just throw it in his general direction."

"I always wondered about that." Roger nodded, fascinated despite himself.

"Nobody up this way!" one of the Cavendishes called outside.

"Nobody up on the roofs!" another called from overhead.

"I still got the feelin' they're around here somewhere," the first voice mused. "Colorado?"

"Right here, California!"

"Why don't you take Ohio and New Mexico and check inside the buildings around here. Michigan, you and Vermont cover them! And why don't you check the feed store first?"

Big Louie brought his six-shooter to eye level.

"Careful now," he whispered to Roger. "This is the big showdown."

Roger swallowed hard. "Okay. This is our moment to be heroes—the big chance for our thrilling victory, right?"

Big Louie grimaced. "Either that—or a double dose of pathos."

CHAPTER

7

That's when the shooting started.

"Hey, California! Who's shoot—Ugh!"

"Colorado! Is that—Ow!"

"Watch out, boys, we don't want to shoot each—AWWWK!"

"Wait a minute! Those bullets are coming from down belo—AURRGGHH!"

"But that would mean it would have to be the town—DROOFF!"

"Are you kidding? It couldn't possibly—BRACCKK!"

Half a dozen miscellaneous screams followed in close succession. Then there was silence.

Louie slid back the bolt on the door and opened it very cautiously.

Doc was sitting up, more or less in the center of a dozen very still bodies. He waved his flask in Louie's general direction.

"I know how to shoot a few Cavendishesh!" he announced before he took another swig. He then promptly collapsed.

"Doc saved us again!" Roger marveled.

"Yeah," Louie agreed. "He must have sobered up barely enough to use his gun. A true son of the West, that Doc." He paused and grinned. "You like that phrase? 'Son of the West.' Gee, it's getting so I can speak real cowboy!"

"So what do we do now?" Roger asked, trying to collect his thoughts.

"I suggest we get out of here, and fast!" Louie said as he waved at the bodies outside. "Sure, we've managed to kill a few of them, but I told you before that the Cavendishes are a *big* gang!" He frowned seriously at Roger. "I think it's time to use your ring."

"My what?" Roger took a step away, tiny alarm bells going off in the back of his brain.

What was this man suggesting? And really, how well did Roger know this fellow, anyway? The one thing Roger did know was that the ring was important—Delores had called it the key to the Cineverse—and if he lost it, he would never see Delores again. Besides that, he wasn't sure how to use the stupid thing. Did he want to admit this to Big Louie, who, up until now, seemed to think Roger was in control of what he was doing? If he brought out the ring, he'd either have to get Big Louie to instruct him in its use, or—if that failed—simply hand the ring over to the sidekick. But could he trust Big Louie to use the ring to save them both? Or would this small fellow dressed in black use the ring for his own nefarious purposes?

There had to be some other way. Didn't there?

"You know," Louie insisted, "your Captain Crusader Decoder Ring. I mean, how else would you have gotten here?"

"Oh," Roger replied, thinking fast. "I see what you mean." Every time he thought about the ring, it seemed more important than the time before. Especially where Delores was concerned. There had to be some way to keep it hidden. Wasn't there?

Louie stared at him expectantly.

"Oh," Roger said again. After a moment, he added: "Well, I have my methods." He hoped it sounded mysterious to Louie. To Roger, it just sounded lame.

"Methods?" Louie's eyes narrowed to calculating slits. "You got here using *methods*? Say, you aren't working for Captain Crusader, are you?"

Amazingly, his ruse seemed to be working! Roger managed to keep a straight face as he replied:

"I am not at liberty to divulge that information."

That was the sort of line you used in public relations when you wanted to confirm everybody's suspicions about something while still being able to claim you were denying them.

"Not at liberty?" Louie grinned. "I should have known. You've got much too much dumb luck for it to be natural. Just about anybody else shows up in town, they'd get gunned down by one side or the other in a matter of seconds!"

Roger smiled to himself. His hastily assembled plan was working better than he could have hoped. Apparently, denizens of the Cineverse had had little exposure to public relations. For the first time since he had shown up in the dust-filled place, he felt he was gaining some control over the situation. But how could he turn all this to his advantage? Or, more to the point, how could he use Big Louie to find Delores?

"But we are wasting time," Roger added decisively. "I have to complete my mission."

"And you said you're not working for Captain Crusader?" Louie laughed. "What do you take me for, anyway?"

Roger decided not to answer that question. Instead, he replied, "We have to rescue Delores."

"Delores?" Louie frowned. "Who's Delores?'

"What? You don't remember Delores?" Roger asked a bit too emotionally. How could this fellow forget the most beautiful woman in the—well, they weren't in the *world* anymore, were they! Very well, then—the most beautiful woman in the Cineverse! Roger took a deep breath. He would have to be careful—he could already feel his control slipping away.

"Hey, I'm sorry." Louie shrugged. "There's an awful lot of women in jeopardy around here. This is the Cineverse, after all!"

"You remember," Roger tried again, forcing patience to take the place of panic. "You must remember. Delores was the woman you came after on my home world? The reason you were holding me at gunpoint?"

"Oh!" Louie brightened. "*That* Delores? You mean the woman Doctor Dread is planning to torture horribly until she reveals all her secrets? Oh, yeah, I remember her now."

Delores? Tortured horribly? Roger found his voice getting more frantic with every word. "Well, I want you to do more than remember her. I want you to help me find her!"

"Oh," Big Louie replied softly, cowering ever so slightly. "She'd be at the hideout—the Devil's Wishbone!"

"The Devil's *Wishbone*?" Roger asked in disbelief.

"Yeah." Louie grinned again. "Pretty neat, huh? Doctor Dread—I mean, Boss Cavendish—always did have a knack for naming hideouts."

But Roger had no more time for neat names. There was an edge to his voice as he asked instead: "Do you know where it is?"

Louie's voice was the slightest bit hurt as he replied. "What do you mean, do I know where it is? Am I a Cavendish or what? Oh. Actually, I'm not a Cavendish anymore, am I? Still, I don't think they would have moved the hideout on account of me. Especially since, as you recall, you and I are currently supposed to have been—uh—taken care of."

"CAN YOU—" Roger interrupted rather loudly.

"I can find it in a pinch," Big Louie hurriedly assured him.

"Well," Roger remarked much more quietly, his breathing once again under control, "the pinch has come."

"What?" Louie exploded in disbelief. "You want us—that is, you and me—you want us to raid the Devil's Wishbone—and rescue this Delores? You want us—two sidekicks if I've ever seen two sidekicks—to go up against the fortifications of Doctor Dread's secret hideaway on this world, fortifications that probably include the rest of the Cavendish gang, and the Cineverse knows what else? You want the two of us to waltz in there past all those guns, rescue this Delores, and then waltz out again? Is that the general idea?"

"Uh, yeah, that was the general idea," Roger admitted.

"How crazy are you?" Big Louie demanded.

"I have my methods," Roger said again. The phrase didn't even sound as good as the last time he had used it.

"Oh, yeah," Louie mused. "Your methods. I keep forgetting—you may be a sidekick, but you're probably Captain Crusader's sidekick! Well, hey, let's use your methods to get us out of here."

Roger shook his head.

"Delores."

Big Louie shook his head. "You really want to go through with this? You are crazy."

Roger decided Big Louie might be right. It probably was crazy to go around acting like a hero in a place like this. But it didn't matter. The only thing that did make any difference was Delores, whether he was back on Earth or on this half-baked movie world. And he was going to get her back, no matter how crazy he had to be.

He stared at Big Louie with such intensity that the small man took another step back.

"Let's look at it this way," Roger began. "You haven't had too much luck as a Cavendish. Do you want to stay in this place for the rest of your life?"

"You mean the Wild West here?" Louie shrugged nonchalantly. "Well, I am learning to speak cowboy." He paused and frowned. "Of course, there's all those Cavendishes who'd like to shoot me." He paused again, pushing at the brim of his ten-gallon hat with his index finger. "Then again, there's all those townspeople, who still think I'm a Cavendish—and probably would like to shoot me even more." He stopped to glance down at the unused gun in his holster. "Well, maybe I could learn to use a six-shooter after all—uh—there must be some way out of here, isn't there?"

"I have my methods," Roger said with what he hoped was a mysterious smile.

Louie sighed. "Well, my methods are your methods. I guess it's time we raided a hideout, huh?"

Roger nodded, satisfied at a job well done. "I'm glad you see it my way. So is this—Devil's Wishbone—around here someplace?"

"Are you kidding?" Louie hooted in disbelief. "Wouldn't be much of a hideout if it was right next door." He frowned, then pointed. "It's out in the desert—thataway."

"Thataway?" Roger asked. "Couldn't you be a little more specific?"

Louie shook his head with finality. "'Thataway' is the only direction allowed out here. Don't you know anything about the Wild West?"

Roger nodded. He kept forgetting he was someplace where only movie logic prevailed.

"Well," Louie remarked with a certain grim finality. "If we're going to get ourselves killed, we might as well get a move on." He stepped from their hiding place into the body-strewn alleyway.

"Okay," Roger answered, trying to sound forceful. He was beginning to wish that the small fellow would sometimes be a little less negative. He glanced at the one body still breathing—and snoring—in the midst of all the other still forms.

"I think it would be a good idea if we took Doc along," he murmured.

"And save him from the outraged excesses of the Cavendishes," Louie replied, "should they find him here and guess the true culprit in the death of all their fellows? Hey—that sounded pretty dramatic, didn't it? I'm getting better and better at this cowboy stuff!" He chuckled appreciatively. "Still, saving Doc, huh? That shows you've got a good heart."

"Yeah," Roger replied. "A heart that I would like to

have continue beating. Hadn't we better get a couple of horses?

"Horses?" Louie mused, glancing at the bodies piled about them. "Shouldn't be any problem. Lot of folks around here won't be needing theirs anymore. Give me a second."

He whistled. Roger heard the sound of pounding hooves. Three horses—complete with saddles, saddle-bags, rifles, canteens, and a few other necessities—galloped into the alleyway.

"Three horses?" Roger asked.

"That's what they are," Louie agreed. "I realize you may be a city boy, and not too familiar with different animals—"

Roger shook his head. "That's not what I meant. Isn't it awfully convenient that when you whistle, the exact number of horses arrive to suit our needs?"

"Hey," Louie retorted. "Anything that moves the plot." He whistled again. "Hey, Lightning!"

A jet-black stallion with a zigzag of white between the eyes reared onto its back legs with a whinny of greeting.

"Now, there's a fine horse," Louie commented. "Used to belong to Dakota, who's recently deceased." He nodded to his left, then turned to Roger. "You do much riding?"

Roger replied that he had been on a horse once or twice when he was fourteen.

"I see," Louie replied doubtfully. "Well, perhaps I should ride Lightning, just to be on the safe side. Now, this other horse here is Tornado."

The second horse, a fiery speckled gray mare, snorted and pawed at the ground, as if it couldn't wait to be galloping somewhere.

"Well," Louie murmured. "Once or twice? Not since fourteen, huh? Hmmm—" He paused to scratch his head. "Maybe we'd better strap Doc to Tornado."

Roger frowned. "Surely there must be some horse I can ride."

"Well, I think you're going to have to work your way up to the likes of Tornado and Lightning," Louie counseled.

"But you're in luck, for the third animal here is my old pony."

A small, nervous white mare shifted from foot to foot. Big Louie stepped over to her, gently patting her flank.

"Roger, this is Modérate Summer Squall."

"Moderate Summer Squall?" Roger exploded before he could help himself. "What kind of name—"

"Well, the Cavendishes were running out of horse names too," Louie replied defensively. "The Cavendishes are a *big* gang. Anyway, I always called her Missy for short."

Roger didn't object. Nervous as Missy seemed, she appeared far less dangerous than either of the larger horses. Maybe if he projected a little confidence, he'd be able to ride her long enough to rescue Delores.

He quickly helped Louie lift Doc and tie him across Tornado's saddle, Doc's arms hanging from one side of the horse, his legs from the other. Doc didn't seem to mind. In fact, Doc didn't seem to wake up at all, except to mumble a slurred "Let'sh shoot shome Cavendishesh. Bang, bang" as they tightened the rope that secured his waist to the saddle. Louie vaulted upon Lightning as Roger gingerly approached Missy. Despite a nervous sidelong glance, Missy allowed Roger to swing up into the saddle.

"Okay!" Louie shouted back to him. "Let's ride!"

All three horses took off at a full gallop. Roger hung on for dear life. This hero business wasn't all it was cracked up to be. Maybe Big Louie was right, and they were destined to never be any more than sidekicks, no matter what they did.

They left the small desert town behind in a matter of moments. Louie slowed the horses' frantic pace down to a steady canter as he scanned the horizon for landmarks, looking, Roger was sure, for "thataway."

Now that he no longer had to hold on for dear life, Roger breathed more easily, allowing himself to rock back in the saddle. Actually, once they had slowed down to this gentler pace, riding a horse was almost pleasant. He had a chance to get a look at the wide-open vistas before him, full of picturesque sagebrush and cacti, a pair of dark brown mesas artfully rising in the distance. The sky above was blue and cloudless, the sun warm on his back, the only sound the horses hooves against the packed earth. Roger almost smiled, reveling in the sudden peace. This was a movie world he could live with.

Thank goodness, Roger reflected, this wasn't one of those singing Westerns, where the hero or his sidekick used the slightest excuse to burst into song about "his Texas Rose" or "these endless prairie skies" or some such. This respite—just the three of them riding through the endless prairie under a Western sky—would finally give Roger a chance to think. Maybe he'd even come up with a way to rescue Delores.

"It is sort of nice out here, isn't it?" Louie remarked, as if he could read Roger's mind. "Especially now that I've figured out which way it is to the Devil's Wishbone. There's only one thing missing."

Louie pointed to Missy's saddlebags.

"Do me a favor—would you?—and hand me that guitar?"

CHAPTER

8

"What's the matter?" Louie asked as he accepted the guitar from Roger's outstretched hand—a guitar that, for some strange reason, Roger hadn't even realized was there until Louie mentioned it. He frowned. How could you miss a guitar?

"You look like you just swallowed your gun," Louie added. "Need to make a rest stop?"

Roger shook his head *no* and asked about what was really bothering him, even though he knew he would hate the answer:

"This isn't one of those singing Westerns, is it?"

Louie grinned as he took a tentative strum. "Oh, you know about this place, do you? Well, my friend, you are in luck, for—in this part of the Cineverse, at least—the West would be nothing without a song." He stretched the fingers of his left hand around the neck of the guitar, and strummed again, producing something slightly off-key. He frowned down at his instrument. "That wasn't quite right, was it?"

Roger could feel the depression settling in already. Not

only was he going to be subjected to songs about Texas roses and the open prairie, he was going to be forced to listen to badly played songs about Texas roses and the open prairie.

Unless he could do something about it. The whole reason the two of them were out on the open prairie about to listen to songs about the same was that Roger had finally taken control of the situation so that he might find Delores at last. Perhaps if he tried exerting his will once again, he could escape this musical assault.

Big Louie mangled an entirely different chord.

"Must you?" Roger complained with as much force as he could muster. "I was enjoying the quiet."

"Sorry, pardner, but I must." Louie pushed back his ten-gallon hat to scratch at his thinning hair. "If I didn't, we'd be stuck in this quiet, endless expanse of prairie forever." He carefully repositioned his fingers on the frets. "Let me explain something to you."

Louie strummed a couple more times on the guitar, the chords sounding almost right. "We were talking before about all the different worlds of the Cineverse having different—even unique—rules, and we've come up against one of those rules here. Under ordinary circumstances it would take us days to ride to the Devil's Wishbone, but when you add a little music, things change—and you find you've reached your goal in under three minutes flat."

He nodded at the great expanses before them. "That's right, it's one of the Laws of the West. All you have to do is sing a song, and, by the time you finish the final chorus, bingo! you've reached your destination. Otherwise it takes forever to get from place to place out here."

"Really?" Roger replied. He supposed it made sense; heaven knew he had seen it happen in Western after Western. It was like all the other laws he had encountered so far in the Cineverse; obvious to a film junkie like himself—if he would have taken a minute to consider it. Apparently, Roger decided, if he was going to survive in this strange, new place, he was going to have to learn to think more like an old movie.

"Besides"—Louie shrugged—"whatever moves the plot along . . ."

He began to strum the guitar with a steady rhythm.

"Now, all I have to remember is one good Western song," Louie mused. "How about this?"

He began to sing. His voice, thankfully, was only slightly flat:

> "Texacali Rose,
> You're wondrin' I suppose,
> Which way the river flows
> And the way the sagebrush grows?
> Could I sniff you with my nose;
> My Texacali—"

Louie stopped himself with a frown.

"That doesn't sound right, does it? I must have gotten the words wrong. Just doesn't have the proper romance." He paused, biting his lower lip for a minute. "Guess I'll have to try another one."

Roger gritted his teeth and decided he would have to suffer through it, for the sake of Delores.

Louie sang and strummed:

> "Out here on the prairie plain,
> A cowboy can make his name;
> Where a man is a man
> and he does what he can;
> And a horse is a horse
> And he does what he's forced,
> But to me now it's all the same!"

"Um," Big Louie paused. "There's a chorus here somewhere. Maybe I'll remember it next time around."

To Roger's regret, he continued his song:

> "Out where the prairie is wide,
> With a six-gun by my side;
> Where a stream is a stream—

It's a watery dream;
And the dirt is the dirt,
It'll get on your shirt,
As you sit in your saddle and ride!"

The small fellow shook his head. "Still can't remember the chorus. You see anything up ahead?"

Roger squinted across the great expanse before them, but, besides an occasional cactus, all he could see were the distant mesas.

"No, luck, huh?" Louie frowned. "Nothing that looks at all like the Devil's Wishbone? And I've already made it through two verses of the song." He sighed. "We'd probably be there already if I could remember the chorus." He shrugged, strumming aimless chords. "Well, perhaps another verse or two."

Louie continued his assault:

"I ride 'cross a prairie that's free,
Wide-open spaces for me:
Where the sky is the sky
And the desert is dry,
And the stars are the stars—
If you squint you'll see Mars,
What a place for a cowboy to be!"

"Are you sure that's the way the song goes?" Roger asked incredulously. This didn't sound like any singing Western song he'd ever heard.

"Shh!" Louie shushed him crossly. "If you break my concentration, we'll never get to the Devil's Wishbone! Let's see now. Oh, yeah, I think I remember . . .

"You'll ride cross the prairie so vast—um—
It's one place that was built to last,
Where a cactus is a cactus
And—er—that's a factus,
And—um—a prairie dog is a prairie dog—"

"Wait a minute!" Roger shouted. "You're making all this up, aren't you?"

"Well, yeah, I ran out of verses," Big Louie admitted. "Was I that obvious?"

"Probably only to a trained ear," Roger replied, backing off slightly when he saw the worry on Louie's face. "Still—"

"I was only trying to help!" Louie complained. "I have to get you to the Devil's Wishbone, so you can get me out of this place before I'm shot by somebody. But its hopeless! The only way we can get to the Devil's Wishbone is if somebody finishes a song!"

But Louie's griping gave Roger an idea. This small ex-Cavendish wasn't the only one around here who knew how to play the guitar. Roger had dabbled with the instrument for a couple of years in college. After all, sensitive numbers like "Fire and Rain"—or anything by Joni Mitchell—had been sure-fire ways to get to meet girls. He still had his old acoustic in a closet somewhere.

"Give that to me!" Roger demanded, pulling the guitar from a surprised Louie's grasp. Of course he hadn't played the guitar in a long time, but surely he'd remember something. He had known a lot of songs in his college days. He strummed experimentally. Then again, he couldn't remember some of those chord changes. Or, for that matter, some of those chords. He frowned, trying to think of some song he could actually make it through.

Only one came to mind. Roger decided it would have to do.

"Shake it up, baby," he began, "twist and shout—"

"Look!" Louie shouted as Roger was singing his final "Oh, yeah!" Roger looked up from his guitar. Their surroundings had totally changed. The mesas, so distant before, towered over them to either side, like two great guardians announcing their entrance into another world. But Louie pointed beyond the mesas. There, in the distance, one corner of a ramshackle hut peaked out of a box canyon.

That, Roger decided, was a definite hideout.

Louie whistled in admiration. "You're not bad at that music stuff, for a city slicker. Why, if you had managed to sneak in a couple references to the open prairie or flowers blooming in some Western state, we would have landed smack dab in the middle of them!"

"Well, I'll work on it," Roger promised, sticking the guitar back in the saddle bags. "Now, however, we have to come up with a plan."

Doc hiccuped loudly.

"A plan?" Louie asked defensively. "Hey, don't look at me. I'm only a sidekick around here."

"Don't worry," Roger replied. "I was only thinking aloud. I'll come up with a plan—somehow." He squinted ahead as they rapidly approached the box canyon. "Actually, it's probably to our advantage that we have a few more minutes of riding ahead of us. It'll give me a chance to think." Like a movie, Roger added to himself, think like a movie. If only he could figure out how the Masked Marshal would handle something like this.

"Hey!" a muffled voice shouted behind him. "What'sh goin' on here?"

Roger looked over his shoulder. From the telltale slur, he realized Doc had revived. From the way the town drunk was squirming about on the saddle, he seemed to have revived in a big way.

"Hey!" Doc exclaimed, fumbling behind his back with the rope that bound his waist to the saddle. "I'm tied to a horshe!"

"Sorry," Roger called. "We didn't think you were sober enough to ride."

"Nonshenshe!" Doc retorted. His hand worried the knots at his belt, his fingers deftly moving their way between the strands of rope until he had pulled every knot apart. As the rope pulled free, he raised himself from the saddle as he grasped the saddle horn, quickly swinging his right leg over the horse as he settled into a sitting positon.

Doc grinned at Roger. "Shober? Shee, I'm perfectly shober."

"My apologies," Roger murmured, quite taken by the performance.

"It'sh nothing," Doc replied modestly. "Jusht a little shomething I learned back when I wash a daredevil rider and eshcape artisht." But his self-satisfied grin turned into a frown as he looked ahead.

"What'sh that?"

"Do you mean the hideout?" Roger offered.

"Chertainly not! I know a hideout when I shee one! What are all theesh dromedariesh doing out here?" Doc demanded. "Or are they camelsh?"

"Oh, dear," Louie remarked softly.

Roger knew just what Louie meant. Doc wasn't going to be much use to anyone if he spent all his time hallucinating. But maybe there was some way to get beyond all this.

"I have no idea what they're doing here," Roger said gently. "However, I think if you will ignore them, they'll ignore you."

"Shage adviche," Doc agreed. "Excushe me." He reached into his coat pocket and retrieved his silver flask. "Jusht one little drink. Shettlesh my nervesh."

Doc drank, three long swallows. He smacked his lips as he recapped the flask.

"That's more like it!" he announced, his voice noticeably stronger.

Something buzzed by Roger's ear—an insect, maybe—although it was traveling awfully fast. Another buzzed past his other ear. Roger wondered absently if they were riding into a swarm of something or other. And then there were those tiny dust clouds rising in front of his horse, as if someone were throwing tiny pebbles into the dirt. But Tornado and Lightning reared up on their hind legs with whinnies of fear. Only Missy continued to plod placidly ahead.

Dust clouds? Traveling awfully fast? Whinnies of fear? Roger frowned. There might be something wrong here.

"Ambush!" Big Louie yelled as he urged his horse toward a nearby cluster of boulders.

Ambush? Roger's frown deepened. That meant these

things flying around him weren't bugs, or even pebbles. They were bullets!

"Somebody's shooting at us?" he asked rather less calmly than he might have wished. Missy turned, sedately following Big Louie's lead behind the clump of rocks.

"Well," Doc replied with a sardonic grin as he swung off his horse. "We'll have to shoot back now, won't we?"

CHAPTER

9

The next few minutes were much too loud for Roger's liking.

There were bullets flying most everywhere, a number of them tearing chunks out of the large cactus immediately above his hiding place. The rock wasn't high enough here for Roger to do much more than kneel and cower. Missy had joined the other two horses behind the much more sensible gigantic boulder that Doc and Big Louie now stood behind. Perhaps, Roger considered, he shouldn't have dismounted quite so quickly. But then, he was new to being shot at.

Roger decided to follow the lead of Doc and Big Louie. He peeked out above his hiding place and lifted his six-shooter, taking the most careful aim that he could, while he was still busy cowering, at one of their dozen or so assailants, most of them hiding in the rocky outcroppings to either side of the box canyon ahead. After the first couple of tries, he managed to keep his gun from jerking wildly in the air as he fired. Once he had cleared that hurdle, he figured he could get aiming down in no time.

By the time he had really gotten the hang of it, however, no one was shooting anymore, and silence once again ruled the desert. In other words, Doc had killed all their opponents.

"Dead?" Louie cried in disbelief. "We got all of them?"

"I think that calls for a drink!" Doc exclaimed.

"Wait a second!" Roger called as he leapt to his feet and ran, with a speed that amazed even himself, to tear the flask from Doc's hand. "We've still got a woman to save. Any celebration now would be far too premature."

"Wow!" Big Louie marveled. "You got a death wish or something? You dare to take a drink away from a gunfighter of Doc's caliber?"

Yes, Roger thought, that was exactly what he'd done. Although he hadn't thought much about the wrath of the gunfighter when he'd done it. He was much more concerned about the unspeakable things Delores might be suffering at this very minute at the hands of Doctor Dread—that, and the fact that Doc seemed to be an excellent gunfighter when he was precisely drunk enough—no more, no less. With too little to drink, the gunfighter was incoherent, with too much, he was unconscious. Roger couldn't let either of those extremes occur, not with Delores' life—actually much more than her life, her *honor*—at stake. That was what he'd been thinking about, and not those other consequences Louie had so helpfully mentioned, when he deprived Doc of a drink. And it was the right decision, too!

Or at least it was as long as Doc didn't shoot him.

"No celebratin' till the job is done?" Doc drawled as he holstered his pistol. "Okay. Sounds like one of the Laws of the West to me."

Well, Roger was glad to get that out of the way. He wiped away the sweat that had suddenly drenched his forehead, and considered their options. The way he saw it, all they had to do now that their presence had been so dramatically announced by the recent gun battle, was to walk into the box canyon, the three of them marching single file down a narrow, well-lit path between two great walls of stone absolutely riddled with the sort of hiding places bad-guy gunmen seemed to favor. It was not an experience Roger was looking forward to.

He looked over at all the black-clad bodies littering the entranceway to the canyon, and had a thought. They would be in trouble—unless, of course, they had managed to shoot all of the Cavendishes. Heaven knew they had managed to shoot a large number of them, even more than he had originally thought. Roger gave up counting when he reached two dozen. Perhaps the worst was over—perhaps there would be no one left inside save Delores and Doctor Dread.

"Louie?" he asked his fellow hopefully. "You don't think, maybe, that we could have shot all of the—"

But Louie shook his head before Roger could finish.

"The Cavendishes are a *big* gang," Louie insisted.

"Well, what are we waitin' for?" Doc chortled manfully. "I hear we've got some rescuin' to do!"

"We're going in there like this?" Louie wailed. "Two sidekicks and a town drunk?"

"No," Roger cuationed. "Wait a minute. I have a plan." At last, he realized, he was beginning to think like an old movie. Louie was already dressed for the part. But both Doc and he needed a change of clothes. After a quick survey of the bodies, he picked the two recently deceased Cavendishes closest in size to Doc and himself, then asked his two companions to give him a hand in stripping the corpses.

"Strip the corpses?" Louie protested. "Haven't you ever heard of death with dignity?"

"I'd rather hear of the three of us surviving what happens next," Roger answered dryly. "We might not have much chance of that as two sidekicks and a town drunk. However, I think our chances improve greatly if we walk into that camp dressed as Cavendishes."

Doc whistled in appreciation. "I gotta hand it to you, stranger, that's a real Western plan."

"But how can it possibly work?" Louie fretted. "They don't know us at all. Won't we still look like strangers?"

Roger shook his head thoughtfully. "There's a chance that won't matter. After all, you said so yourself: The Cavendishes are a *big* gang."

Reluctantly, Louie helped Doc and Roger get the clothes off the corpses, then left to tie the horses out of sight. By the time he returned, all three of them were dressed in black.

Louie sighed, still not convinced. "We may look like Cavendishes, but to me we still feel like two sidekicks and a town drunk."

Doc chuckled in return. "Come on now. Is that any way to look into the jaws of danger?"

"No," Louie admitted. "It's only my way. Actually, I would much prefer to look into the jaws of danger from a somewhat greater distance—say, back in town?" He smiled apologetically.

"Come on," Roger said. "Let's get this over with." The two silver six-shooters he had strapped to his waist felt cold against his palms as he slowly made his way toward the entrance to the canyon. Deep in his heart he felt almost as uneasy as Big Louie, for he realized he was probably leading all three of them into certain death. But if he didn't, then what would happen to Delores? Unless it was already too late. He pushed the thought from his mind, concentrating on the sounds of six spurs a'jangling as the three of them trudged down the incline to the canyon floor.

He had to face up to it. What happened next was going to be dangerous. It might be downright impossible.

It also didn't help that the boots he was now wearing were a little tight.

"Yo!" called a voice from the canyon wall. "Who goes there?"

Roger stopped and swallowed, even though his mouth was desert dry. If they could fool the guard, they could get in to rescue Delores. If not—

Roger refused to think the rest of that thought. He saw Doc's hand edge over to brush against his pearl-handled revolver. Roger shook his head. It was time to use cunning, not force. He stared at the ground as he called up to the sentry, doing his best to keep his face hidden in the shadow of his hat.

"Cavendishes coming in!" he called. That was the sort of thing bad guys said when they walked into a secret hideout, wasn't it?

"Cavendishes?" the sentry began. "What's the pa—"

"Don't worry," a gruff cowboy voice said from up ahead. "I'll show 'em around."

"Okay! You're the boss!" The sentry disappeared behind an outcropping of rock.

Roger turned to the other Cavendish, several yards ahead. He was the biggest bad guy Roger had seen so far, a full three inches taller than the recently deceased California. He smiled at Roger and his companions, and Roger saw that three of his teeth were gold. When he smiled, he looked even meaner. Maybe, Roger considered, it was because of all those scars.

"Follow me, pardners," the very large man remarked right after he spat. The spittle landed on the toe of Roger's borrowed boot, a distance, Roger realized, of some twenty feet. Roger looked up at the large man, but he had already turned around and was walking away.

"Welcome to the Devil's Wishbone," the immense fellow called over his shoulder. Roger could see the fellow's back muscles ripple as he moved, even under his black shirt. "I'm the foreman around here."

"Foreman?" Roger asked before he could stop himself. Did a hideout need a foreman?

"Every place in the Old West needs a foreman," the foreman rumbled. "It's one of the Laws of the West. There's certain laws even bad guys don't break."

"Sure, we knew all about that," Louie hastily added.

Doc's hand hung nervously over his gun. His free hand reached toward the pocket with the flask, but Roger again shook his head emphatically.

Roger couldn't blame his fellows. Even he had to admit that this newest Cavendish tended toward the sinister. Still, what else would you expect from a foreman of the bad guys? At least his plan was working, and they were getting inside the Devil's Wishbone. In fact, it had been far easier than he first imagined.

"I figured you boys, bein' new here and all, would like a look around," the foreman drawled with a chuckle. "This up ahead is the main house."

"The main house?" Roger blurted before he could cover his mouth. The place up ahead looked like nothing more than a weathered, unpainted shack—the sort of place that when you opened the door, you fully expected the roof to cave in.

"Sounds better than the main shack," the foreman explained. "This is a hideout, after all. In this business you gotta make some compromises."

A man in a black snakeskin hat appeared on the inside of a dust-smeared window for an instant. It had to be Doctor Dread! Roger's breath caught beneath his Adam's apple—that meant Delores was inside for sure! As if to confirm his suspicions while they approached the shack, Roger could hear voices arguing inside.

"So what do *you* want to do with her?" a woman's voice demanded.

"Oh," Doctor Dread's slimy voice replied. "I don't know. Something"—he paused significantly—"appropriate."

"But there are so many options!" the woman's voice insisted. "I mean, there's tying her to the railroad tracks, or chaining her to a log that's about to go through the sawmill, or how about stranding her in a boat that's just about to go over the waterfall?"

"Aren't those a little"—Dread paused meaningfully—"too common? We want her to"—he halted tellingly—"talk, after all."

"I see. You want me to be a little more"—she hesitated knowingly—"creative."

"Yes, we need something to make her"—he stalled suggestively—"especially cooperative."

"Oh!" the woman responded brightly. "Why didn't you say so? Why not strap her out in the desert sun, her hands and feet bound by strips of wet rawhide which will shrink

painfully as they dry, her face smeared with honey and sure
to attract those fire ants milling around that anthill close by
her left ear, bits of a sacred totem broken and scattered
about her helpless form, sure to infuriate that fierce band of
renegade Indians that have just appeared on yonder hill—"

Roger couldn't stand this anymore! They were talking
about torturing the woman he loved! He ran forward.

"Oh," the foreman drawled without the least surprise.
"You want to look around inside, do you? Well, at least let
me open the door."

He did precisely that, and Roger rushed into the shack.
Doctor Dread looked up as he entered the room. Standing
nearby was a woman Roger had never seen before, an imposing female of a height equal to or greater than that of
the foreman who had led them here.

But all thoughts of the others fled as he saw who was
bound and gagged in a chair between those two, her perfect
face illuminated by a kerosene lamp at her feet. Hope lit
her eyes as she saw him enter the room. His plan had
worked after all. They had found Delores!

"Who is it?" Doctor Dread's voice held the slightest
note of annoyance. "More members of our"—he paused
significantly—"little family?"

Their large guide grunted in reply. "No, actually it's two
sidekicks and a town drunk. But they're dressed like Cavendishes. I thought I'd bring them around to you before
we shot them."

Shot them? Perhaps, Roger considered, his plan still had
a few flaws. He glanced behind him, ready to bolt at the
slightest opportunity. Doc and Big Louie were crowded
close by his back. And in the doorway—their only possible means of escape—stood the foreman, the same foreman who had drawn both his revolvers and was covering
all three men.

"Shoot them?" Dread frowned disapprovingly. "Oh, no,
no, no."

"What?" The foreman's gold-toothed grin faltered. "We
shouldn't shoot them?"

Dread wiggled a finger in the large cowboy's direction.

"No, no, you should never *talk* about shooting them. People like this should be"—he paused significantly—"removed. They should be"—he paused—"dispensed with. These matters have to be discussed with"—yet another pause—"some delicacy."

The big fellow shook his head slowly, struggling to comprehend.

"Then, of course, once you're done implying things, you can take them out and shoot them," Dread added. "It's as simple as that. You have a lot to learn, Ontario, about being a Cavendish."

"Ontario?" Roger asked, unable to stop himself.

"He's from the northern branch of the gang," explained Dread with an oily grin.

Roger did his best to manage his breathing. It would do him no good to panic now, and he didn't want to think what would happen to Delores if he lost control. So what if his first plan hadn't quite worked? All he had to do was think like a movie. What did he remember about the Wild West on film?

Yeah, Roger thought, the plots of a dozen B-Westerns flying through his mind. You could always talk or fight your way out of trouble with bad guys. Well, you could, that is, if you were the hero. Roger wasn't sure if the rule held up for sidekicks. Still, it was worth a try.

"But wait a minute!" Roger insisted. "What are you guys talking about? We're Cavendishes!"

"Sure," Ontario the foreman chortled. "And I'm the first robin of spring."

Doctor Dread and the very imposing female shared in the laughter.

"Oh, yeah? Well—um—er—oh, yeah?" Roger countered none too steadily. Perhaps words weren't going to work after all. But that meant they were going to have to use their fists, didn't it? Roger wished some of the bad guys weren't quite so tall. Maybe he just hadn't talked enough. "Don't we look like Cavendishes?"

All the bad guys roared at that one.

"Give it up," Big Louie cautioned. "They know who I am!"

"Oh," Roger remarked. He should have thought of that, Big Louie having been in Dread's gang and all. "You mean Doctor Dread remembers—"

"How could he forget?" Louie stared down at his tooled leather boots. "You see that statuesque woman over there? She's my sister."

The statuesque woman grinned and approached them. The floorboards shook beneath her feet as she walked. She stuck out her hand in Roger's direction.

"Put 'er there. You can call me Bertha. You know, for a sidekick, you're kind of cute."

Hesitantly, Roger took her hand. Once she had let go, Roger shook his hand again in an attempt to restart the blood flow.

"Bertha," she repeated with a smile that implied all sorts of things Roger didn't want to think about. "My friends call me—Big Bertha. Remember the name. I think I'm going to be seeing"—she paused in that way the bad guys had—"a lot of you."

Roger swallowed, his throat even dryer than it had been in the desert. What did she mean by that? And why did her tone give Roger a queasy feeling deep down in his stomach?

"Alas, dear Bertha," Dread interrupted unctuously, "I fear we don't have time for that. These poor unfortunates must be—dealt with."

"Oh, yeah?" Doc erupted, spinning abruptly and felling the large Cavendish behind him with one well-aimed blow of his fist. Ontario crashed to the parched earth outside the shack. Doc turned again and staggered forward so that he stood at Roger's side. He grinned at the remaining bad guys.

"You want to bet on that?"

"Yeah," Roger agreed as his fingers curled reassuringly around the cool handle of his revolver. "I think we're going to leave here with what we came for." He smiled reassuringly at the hogtied love of his life.

"Delores!" Roger called.

"Mmmmppphhhffff!" Delores replied. Roger's smile broadened. It was wonderful to hear the sound of her voice again. Her fashionable silver bracelets clinked together as she tried to turn toward him, but she was so securely bound she could do nothing save clink her silver bracelets. This was too much for him to take! He took a step forward.

"No." Doc placed a restraining hand on Roger's shoulder. "Let me do it. You never know what tricks these Cavendishes are up to."

Roger nodded and stepped aside. He was happier with every passing moment that he had kept Doc from taking that extra drink. It was amazing how capable the fellow was when he wasn't falling-down inebriated. Now, Roger was sure, as long as they kept Doc on the wagon, they'd be able to free Delores and foil anything the Cavendishes could throw at them.

Doc sauntered forward, his spurs a'jangling over the rotting floorboards.

"We'll have you out of this in a minute, missy," Doc murmured nobly as he approached. "Excuse me while I move this lamp." He squatted in front of Delores' chair and dragged the kerosene lantern toward him, making a face as the fumes hit his nose.

"Excuse me," he muttered. "I'll untie you just—" He blinked rapidly, his face taking on a vaguely unfocused look. "Excushe—" he started again. "I'll untie you— right"—his eyes seemed to cross of their own accord— "after I jusht take a little nap!"

Doc was snoring before he hit the floor. Maybe, Roger reflected, it had been an alcohol lantern. Whatever—it took Roger but an instant to realize Doc's inhaling of the fumes had once again driven him over the edge. This was terrible! All was lost, unless he and Big Louie could act quickly.

"Stay where you are!" Roger barked as he quickly pulled his revolver from his holster to cover Doctor Dread and Bertha. He figured this was his last chance to get the drop on the bad guys, while they were still surprised by recent events. And even later he would still agree that his theory was near perfect movie-thinking. Still, he had to admit it probably would have been much more effective had the gun not flown out of his hand the minute he yanked it from its holster. He heard it clatter in the far corner of the room at the same instant he felt something hard pressing into the small of his back.

"You're pretty good at throwing away your gun," Ontario drawled. "Now let's see how good you are at throwing away your life."

"What a great line!" Dread enthused. "Do I know how to pick my foremen, or what?"

"Well, Boss?" Roger heard the twin clicks of two gun hammers behind him. "Is it time?"

"Soon, Ontario, very soon," Dread assured his crony. He smirked at Roger. "I could have him—deal with you —right away. But no, I think that first I shall—spend a minute and gloat over my—master plan! That's right. I have only begun to tear down those fences and stampede my cattle over the properties of innocent homesteaders! And only today did we burn down the Assayer's Office so we could jump the claims of unsuspecting prospectors. Now, after we alter the river's course to control the water rights and make preparations for the railroad to come through—" He paused to laugh maniacally. "And that's only on this world, a small part of my—master master plan!"

"Can I deal with them now, Boss?" Ontario asked hopefully.

"Roger?" Big Louie's voice quavered at his side.

Roger turned to look at his companion. Could the small man know of some way out of this?

Louie's smile faltered as he added, "It's been good knowing a sidekick as nice as you."

Sidekick? Roger guessed that answered his question. He had come to this world trying to be a hero, but would end up as pathos. He guessed it was fate.

"Wait!" the tall woman commanded. "There may be another way."

A flicker of hope stirred deep within Roger. He had forgotten that this big woman was Big Louie's sister! Maybe family feelings could save them where all else failed!

"Now, now, Bertha," Doctor Dread chided. "I know one of these sidekicks is your brother—"

"That's not it at all!" Bertha interjected. "I was foolish in talking you into giving Seymour—or whatever he calls himself now—a job. Let's face it—my brother should have been shot a long time ago. No, I want the other one." She smiled thinly in Roger's direction. "I thought he was cute before, but when he ineptly tried to take control a moment ago, it sent shivers down my spine. That's when I knew he had to be mine."

Bertha paused to make grasping motions with her very large hands. "I haven't *used* anybody in ever so long!"

Roger would have taken a step away if he hadn't had a gun stuck against his spine. The way this woman was looking at him through those half-closed eyelids started him thinking how simple and clean death could be.

"Now, now, Bertha—" Dread began.

"Oh, I know it means keeping him alive a little while longer," Bertha pleaded. "But think of it this way. When I'm done, there won't be much left of him, will there? I mean, by that point, his being alive will be more of a technicality."

"No, Bertha," Dread said with finality. "As long as this interloper lives, there would be a small chance he might escape, and even though, being with you, it would probably take him months to recover, I still can't take that chance. They will have to be—dealt with—now."

Ontario chuckled behind Roger. "Oh, boy! Does that mean it's time?"

"Yes," Dread agreed gleefully. "You put it so well. It is—hehheh—time."

This was it, then. Roger's throat was so dry he didn't

even try to swallow. He looked a final time at Delores as she bravely tried to blink the tears from her eyes. At least he had seen her a final time before the end. There was no way to save them now.

That's when he heard the bugle.

CHAPTER

⟁ 10 ⟁

A bugle? But it couldn't be!

"Drat!" Doctor Dread cursed. "It's the cavalry!"

Then it was a bugle! Come to think of it, Roger reconsidered, in a place like this it was not only possible, it was probably required.

"Thank goodness!" Louie whispered at his side. "We're going to be rescued by one of the Laws of the West."

"Movie Magic?" Roger whispered back.

Louie nodded. "Hey!" he remarked a second later. "Maybe this means we're not sidekicks after all. Or— maybe—*one* of us isn't a sidekick!"

Louie and Roger frowned at each other.

"Aw, come on, Boss," Ontario pleaded. "Can't I deal with these guys anyway?"

"Now, now," Dread reprimanded, "you've been on Western worlds long enough to know what would happen if we attempted that! Oh, sure, it would begin promisingly enough. You'd lead these two out into the sun outside the shack. Then, with an evil smile spread across your face as you simultaneously pulled back the triggers of your two six-shooters so you could plug both these sidekicks dramatically at the same time, the heroic leader of the cavalry would ride over a nearby hill, and, with a single shot, fire a bullet past your spine and straight into your heart, causing your two guns to fire harmlessly in the air as you fell, lifeless, into the desert sand."

"Oh, yeah." Ontario pondered. "I guess that would happen, wouldn't it?"

Dread nodded solemnly. "It's one of the Laws of the West."

"You mean," Bertha blurted, "that I won't have any time to *use* him?" From the way she smiled hungrily at Roger, there was no doubt who she was referring to.

"Alas," Dread replied sadly, "I am afraid for now that all our desires must go"—he paused significantly—"unfulfilled."

"Maybe just a little?" Bertha winked in Roger's direction. "With my techniques, I assure you it will take no time at all."

"That, unfortunately, is exactly what we have," Dread said with finality. "No time at all."

"But can't we do anything?" Ontario asked, hands still hopefully on his gun handles.

Dread nodded curtly. "We can get out of here." He waved to his fellows. "Bertha, Ontario, I need each of you to hold onto a sleeve of my fringe jacket."

Dread's cronies did as they were instructed, Bertha somehow managing it without looking away from Roger.

"Good," Dread commended his fellows. "Now I want each of you to place a hand on the shoulder of our captive."

"Mmmmpphhh!" Delores protested.

"Delores!" Roger cried in despair, unable to cope with the thought of his one true love once again being snatched away to parts unknown.

"How magnificently pitiful!" Bertha said, her voice a low, throaty growl. "Couldn't we find a way to take this one along?" Her tongue darted across her teeth in anticipation. "I promise to use him very quietly! You'll hardly even hear his pleas for mercy—really!"

But Dread frowned at her suggestion. "No. There is something about this newcomer that seems to upset any plan we may devise. If we cannot kill him—and I assure you, should one of us even attempt it at this moment, we would be destroyed where we stood—then we must disappear somewhere where he can never follow us, so that we may complete our plans and destroy his kind forever!"

"But can't he follow us—" Bertha insisted, "if he has a ring?"

"An excellent point!" Dread mused. "Then there is one final thing we must do before we—take our leave. Ontario, point your guns at Louie."

Ontario grinned. "That's more like it, Boss!"

Shots rang outside of the shack. Somebody screamed as he fell a considerable distance. The bugle blew again.

"They got the lookout!" Bertha exclaimed.

"Yes," Dread replied. "We have no time to lose. Ontario, unless Louie tells us where his friend is hiding the Captain Crusader Decoder Ring, shoot him."

Ontario frowned. "But I thought you said—"

"That only applies to heroes," Dread interrupted. "There's some possibility this Roger is one of those. That's why we're not pointing the gun at him. Louie, on the other hand, is lucky to be even considered a sidekick. I think we just have time to shoot him before we escape."

"Oh, boy, a shooting!" Ontario enthused. "Can I do it now?"

"In a second," Dread cautioned. "After all, we need to give him a little time to spill his guts. It's one of the Laws of the West."

"Okay, small stuff." Ontario cocked both his pistols. "The ring or a bullet. Which is it going to be?"

"But—but—" Big Louie was sweating so profusely, his hat threatened to slide down to cover his eyes. "Y-you can't shoot me!"

"Wanna bet?" Ontario's fingers curled around twin triggers.

The hat fell over the top of his nose as Louie vehemently shook his head. "Y-you don't understand. R-r-roger doesn't have a r-ring—"

"Doesn't have a ring?" Dread demanded. "Are you sure—?"

"But that means—" Bertha announced as respect mixed with lust in her gaze.

"It means we should kill him anyway!" Ontario turned his guns toward Roger.

Somebody pounded heavily on the door as the bugle blew on the other side of the window.

"Open up!" a gruff voice announced. "It's the cavalry!"

"Too late!" Dread cried. "To my side, Ontario. We leave this instant!"

Ontario and Bertha resumed their positions, forming a circle with Dread and Delores.

"Mmmmmppphhhh!" Delores protested a final time.

"Don't worry," the Doctor sneered in Roger's direction. "We'll be back . . . once the laws have changed!"

He twisted the plastic ring on his finger.

"See you in the funny papers!"

The four of them were surrounded by blue smoke, and then they were gone.

Only one word escaped from Roger's lips:

"Delores!"

There had to have been some way he could have saved her. Dread had told his henchperson not to kill him, after all, although Ontario had seemed ready to shoot him at the slightest provocation right until the very end. But would they have dared to do anything? The cavalry had shown up, and Louie swore they only came around when there was a hero to rescue. And Dread had assured Louie that he could never ever be a hero, which, by the process of elimination, meant that the hero had to be Roger. Didn't it? But if he was the hero, he should have been able to rescue Delores. Shouldn't he? Then, to confound things, she had disappeared in a puff of smoke, and he was still standing here, doing nothing in particular while the cavalry made a lot of noise with their bugles outside. Is that the sort of thing a hero would do?

Roger had to admit it: He was confused.

And then the cavalry broke down the door.

A burly man dressed in cavalry blue, his dusty uniform sporting sergeant's stripes upon the sleeve, was the first into the shack.

"Where is he?" the newcomer demanded.

"Where's who?" Louie asked. "Didn't you come to save us?"

Slim, or possibly Sam, strode through the door next. Whichever one he wasn't followed at the first one's heels.

"There he is!" One of the two pointed at the still-snoring form of Doc, curled up in the middle of the uneven floor.

A number of other cavalry members, along with some miscellaneous townspeople, piled into the shack as well. Somebody blew a bugle in Doc's ear.

"What? Huh?" Doc yawned and stretched, squinting up at the room full of people. "Can't a fellow get a dechent afternoon'sh shleep around here?"

The townspeople cheered.

"That's our Doc!" Bart said cheerfully.

"Yeah," Bret joined in. "It's nice to have him back. Sagebrush just wasn't the same without our town drunk!"

"Wait a moment!" Roger interjected. "That's why you're here? To rescue the town drunk?"

"Sure!" Bart replied. "Why else would we come out to a goshforsaken place like this? You only use the cavalry when it's a life and death situation."

Bret whistled in agreement. "You can't underestimate the importance of a town drunk! I tell you, sitting in a bar without someone groveling in the sawdust for drinks simply isn't the same."

Bart nodded. "Takes all the fun out of a town. But that's all gonna change, now that we have our drunk back. Sam, Slim, why don't you help Doc out to the horses?"

"Excuse me," Roger interrupted once again, still not truly believing the import of all this, "but—rescuing Doc —that's the only reason you came out here?"

"Sure." Bart chuckled. "No offense, but do you think we'd waste the cavalry's time on rescuing a couple of side-kicks?"

Doc sat up and blinked at the two men trying to help him to his feet. "Hey! Wait a minute! What are you doing out here?"

"Why," replied Slim or Sam—whichever one it was who still had his arm in a sling, "we're here to rescue you."

"Now that's not what I mean, and you know it! I cut a bullet out of you a few hours ago, and here you are riding all over the desert." Doc shook his grizzled head in disgust. "I swear, Sam, I don't know why I bother!"

"Uh, pardon me, Doc," the man in the sling replied, "but I'm Slim."

"Hey!" his companion added rapidly. "Are you sure of that?"

Slim frowned. "What do you mean?"

"Well, I don't know how to tell you this—" His fellow cleared his throat. "I always thought I was Slim."

Maybe-not-Slim blanched beneath his deep Western tan. "Then that means I'm Sam?"

The other nodded.

Roger couldn't believe this. "Aren't *either* of you sure?"

"Well—" the one in the sling began.

"No," the slingless one finished.

"You know, life out here in the Old West gets a mite wearyin'—" Maybe-Sam continued.

Maybe-Slim added, "What with a heavy-duty life of cow punchin' and poker playin', some of these little distinctions get lost."

Possibly-Sam shrugged. "Yeah, you know, a fella gets confused."

"We once thought about getting tattoos," Possibly-Slim admitted. "But, you know, it gets embarrassing, having to peek inside your shirt all the time to see if it's really you they're talking to."

Roger nodded. Somehow, the explanation of these two

cowpokes had left him even more thoroughly confused than he had been before. Still, perhaps because of his public relations training, or perhaps because he wanted to interrupt Slim and Sam's never-ending ramblings, he felt he had to say something.

"I never realized it was so bad," he said sympathetically.

"That's not the half of it!" one of the two complained. "You should see the problem we have with our wives."

"Well, I'm sure you folks are havin' a fine time gettin' reacquainted," Bart interrupted in his characteristic drawl, "but I think it's about time we got Doc back to town."

"Yeah!" Bret chimed in, bending down over the still-seated object of their rescue. "Say, Doc, would you like a little nip to get you back on your feet?"

But Doc shook his head. "I've decided to give up nippin'—and drinkin' too—for the time bein'. Now, help me up, would you?"

Startled into silence, Bart did as he was told.

"Appreciate it," Doc said. "Now let's get goin'."

Both cavalry and townfolk followed Doc from the shack. The last one out—who was probably Sam, depending upon who you believed—glanced over his shoulder as he stood on the threshold, and spoke to Roger and Louie.

"Oh, I guess it's all right if you guys come along, too. With all the dead Cavendishes out there, there's bound to be some extra horses."

"I guess we'd better go," Louie said after a second, quickly following the last cowboy out.

Roger left the shack as well, stepping out into a chaotic mass of men and horses. He didn't know what he should do next, but he didn't particularly want to be left behind.

Still, what was the use of going anywhere? Apparently, he wasn't a hero after all, but had been forced into the role of permanent sidekick on this strange new world. That meant nobody would ever pay much attention to him, with the possible exception of another sidekick like Big Louie.

That thought alone was depressing enough. More important, though, if he was nothing but a sidekick, how could he possibly rescue Delores?

"Hurry up!" Louie called back to him. "The others are leaving!"

Roger started running, hoping he could find Missy somewhere in the milling crowd before him.

CHAPTER

⚐ 11 ⚐

Somehow, Roger managed to find his horse. Somehow,
even more miraculously, he managed to mount his horse
and ride after the others.

He was getting over the shock of not being a hero, and
other things entered his mind. Other things like how could
he get out of this place to rescue Delores. He still had the
ring, after all. He simply had no idea how to use it.

Maybe he should have stayed back at the Devil's Wishbone, and tried to follow Doctor Dread from there. But
even Roger had to admit that the only thing that had gotten
him this far was stubbornness and pure dumb luck. He had
somehow managed to copy the exact ring setting Big Louie
had used in order to follow him here. But that wouldn't
work again. He had been too busy staring helplessly at
Delores—she really was beautiful, even when she was
bound and gagged—to really get a good look at Doctor
Dread's adjustments to his personal key to Cineverse.
Without knowing the proper ring setting, how could Roger
hope to follow?

Unless Big Louie knew where they might have gone.

Roger sighed. Maybe he should confide in the small side-kick after all. And why not? Louie had stood by his side during their entire confrontation with the Cavendish gang. The black-clad sidekick was loyal and steadfast and ever-dependable, just like companions in the movies, especially Western movies. Roger was startled to realize that Louie might even be considered a friend. Not only that, but, with Delores gone, Louie was his only friend in the Cineverse.

The rest of the riders were far ahead, cloistered around the still-sober Doc. The whole rescue party, some thirty or forty strong, seemed to collectively care less whether or not Roger and Louie tagged along. In a way, Roger re-flected, the crowd's indifference gave the two of them some much needed privacy for discussion of important things, like rescuing Delores, and confessing that Roger did, indeed, possess a ring.

"Louie," Roger began. "I've got to talk to you about something."

"So you felt it, too?" Louie replied before Roger could launch into his appeal. "There's something very wrong here."

"Of course there's something wrong!" Roger insisted. "They've captured Delores."

"Oh, that's true, too." Big Louie murmured distractedly. He snapped his fingers. "I know what's bothering me. Re-member what Dread said as he left—that he'd be back when the laws were—different? What did he mean by that? Nobody can change the Laws of the West. Can they?"

Roger still didn't know enough about this place to give him an answer.

Apparently, Louie didn't really need one, because he kept on talking. "It would mean a complete realignment of the very forces that move the Cineverse—or perhaps—something even worse!" He frowned at his fellow sidekick. "You've heard about the Change?"

Roger nodded, surprised at the intensity of Louie's re-sponse.

"The Change? Delores mentioned it to me once. She

didn't really have any time to explain it, though, before you guys showed up to kidnap her."

"Oh, that." Louie blushed. "Well, I was only doing my job, you know. If only I had realized the implications of Dread's plans! And here I was, trying to change my lot in life—Oh, if only I had stayed in comic relief!" Without letting go of the reins, Louie still managed to wring his hands melodramatically.

"You were talking about the Change?" Roger prompted helpfully.

"Oh. Sure. The Change. Right." He took a deep breath, trying desperately to compose himself. "It was a while ago now, perhaps a couple decades past by the methods you—on that planet of yours—tell time. Nobody was quite sure how it began, although some did expect Doctor Dread had a hand in it—but if he did, it was probably in another one of his guises. Oh, I should have realized that before I became involved with him! But no, I was tired of pratfalls, and looking for variety—"

Roger cleared his throat. "The Change?"

"Oh." Louie smiled apologetically. "Yeah. So, anyway, things began to unravel everywhere in the Cineverse. It was small stuff at first, an extraneous death among the supporting characters here, an unresolved subplot there. But it escalated quickly. There came a dark time when it seemed that every hero had to die!"

Roger's breath caught at the back of his throat. Twenty years ago, Louie had said? He remembered that time, in the late sixties and early seventies, in every movie he would go to see—whether it was a Western, a cop movie or a motorcycle flick—where the hero would be blown away by excessive gunfire thirty seconds before "The End" showed up on the screen. It had been a dark time indeed. A shiver shook Roger's shoulders and spine. So that was the Change?

"Only the greatest of heroes was able to stem that horrible tide," Louie continued. "Imagine! World after world where solutions to disasters come a moment too late, where boy always loses girl never to find her again, and the bad guys get away every time?"

Disasters? Lost love? The bad guys always win? Roger had to admit it sounded terrible. It also sounded all too familiar. That was the way things always happened on Earth, every day, in real life, not in the movies! Roger shivered. The Change was far worse than he could have imagined.

"And Dread planned all this?" Roger asked.

"In one of his guises, it is very likely that he did. At least, that's what I suspect. You've seen Dread in action. Have you ever seen anyone so evasive? I mean, how could you possibly pin anything on someone who is always pausing meaningfully like that? Oh, why didn't I remember that before I took the job?" Louie gripped his reins so fiercely, his knuckles turned the color of bone. "I was desperate to get out. I was in comedy relief for years! I mean, can you imagine going through plot after plot and never *ever* getting the girl?"

"So Dread is responsible for all this? The fiend!" Roger took a deep breath in an attempt to control his outrage. "But his plan failed, didn't it? The Cineverse is still working, isn't it?"

"Well—" Louie hesitated. "Yes and no," he said at last. "The Cineverse is still here, and the plots go on, after a fashion. But some of those things that fell apart before were never put back together, and some plot lines seem to have unraveled for good. I mean, look at our situation here. We got all the classic plot twists—a damsel in distress, a last-minute rescue by the cavalry—but what does the cavalry come to rescue? Not the damsel, and not a hero. No, they've rescued the town drunk! That would never have happened in the classic Cineverse!"

Roger frowned, trying to comprehend everything Big Louie was telling him. "But what does all this have to do with Delores?"

"Delores?" Louie frowned back. "Who's De—Oh, that's right. There's just so many distressed damsels, you know—She must fit in somehow. Maybe she was one of those sent outside to get help. Or maybe she had been working for Doctor Dread, too, had tried to double-cross him." He shrugged when he saw Roger's outraged response to his last statement. "How should I know? I'm only a sidekick!"

Roger told himself to calm down once again. What, after all, did he really know about Delores—besides the fact that she was the most beautiful, intelligent, vivacious, and witty woman he had ever met? Then again, his overall track record with women hadn't been all that wonderful. Just look at what had happened with Wendy. And he still had trouble thinking about Cynthia, especially whenever he ate Chinese food!

But he had forgotten all those other women when he met Delores. She had seemed to genuinely like him for who he was, even encouraged some of his personality traits—traits that previous girlfriends and wives had listed as his faults. Still, she had been so mysterious about most of her past. Could she have been hiding the very sort of thing Big Louie suggested? Could she be a beautiful, vivacious, intelligent, and witty bad guy?

Roger realized it didn't matter. He loved her, no matter what. He wouldn't believe that she was evil, mean, rotten, and nasty until she had told him to his face, and, even then, he might stick around a little while to see if she would change her mind. Oh, sure, he had had a similar experience with Eunice, and even now he didn't like to think of what had happened with Marilyn. But that was different. Neither of them—in fact, none of his earlier wives or girlfriends—had come from the Cineverse.

He would go on then, and rescue Delores, even if it meant turning every corner of the Cineverse upside down to succeed! Or, at least he would as soon as he figured out what he should do next.

"Yeah," Big Louie replied, although Roger hadn't spoken. "I'm wondering what to do, too. Whatever's going on here, we seem to be right in the middle of it. Does this mean anything?"

The small man lifted his index finger aloft, his eyes shining with inspiration.

"Maybe we are destined to do great things!"

He blinked, and the shining inspiration suddenly seemed a lot more like the reflection of the desert sun.

"Then again," he added much more quietly, "maybe we are two sidekicks, way over our heads."

Roger didn't know what to say. After a moment, he asked his question anyway:

"So what should we do now?"

"It probably wouldn't be a bad idea to catch up with the others," Louie suggested. "They seem to be cantering faster than we are."

"No," Roger replied. "That's not really what I meant. I was thinking more in terms of what we should do to—well—rescue Delores and possibly the Cineverse."

Louie nodded grimly. "Big talk for a sidekick. Still, if that's the way you feel about it, there's only one thing we can do. Whether we are more important than we realize, or mere cogs in the great wheel that powers the Cineverse, we have to find Captain Crusader!"

"Captain Crusader!" Roger exclaimed despite himself. *The* Captain Crusader? The namesake of the decoder rings, the speaker of noble thoughts such as "The four basic food groups are your friends" and "A clean plate is a happy plate"? He had never thought of it before, but if the Captain Crusader Decoder Ring was real, that meant Captain Crusader had to exist as well, didn't it?

"Of course," Louie replied smoothly. "Captain Crusader is the hero's hero. He appears from time to time throughout the Cineverse. I believe you've seen him once already."

"I have?" Roger replied in disbelief. Then he remembered.

It was so obvious. Why hadn't he realized it before? That was why the Masked Marshal had looked so familiar. And why that civic slogan he had uttered had sent a chill down Roger's spine.

"But," Roger said, "there's one thing I don't understand. If Captain Crusader—that is, the Masked Marshal

—is the hero's hero, why did he leave Sagebrush before the gun battle?"

"Yep," Big Louie replied. "That's something that worries me too. Maybe the Change is spreading once again."

Louie looked at the distant rescue party and whistled. "But we've got other things to worry about. Doc is pulling out a guitar!"

"Does Doc sing, too?"

Louie nodded. "We have to assume the worst. I've got the feeling Doc could do anything, if he stays sober. But there's a hitch here—we've gotta join that singing party up ahead right pronto. If we're not within easy listening range of the singer, we'll be left days away from Sagebrush! Hurry!"

The music drifted faintly their way as Roger urged his slow-moving horse to greater speed. He recognized a word here and there in the song, something about a "pretty prairie flower" and a reference to the "wide-open skies of Arizona."

By the time Roger got Missy into a gallop, Doc had made it to the chorus. The sound swelled as the other members of the rescue party joined in.

"Oh, no!" Big Louie shouted. "They're singing together! That's going to make the magic work all that much faster!" He glanced back at Roger, holding his own mount back so that his fellow sidekick could catch up.

"Maybe," Louie suggested, "if we sing along, it'll work for us, too." And with that, he burst into hesitant song. "With my six-gun by my side, on—um—my saddle I will ride—um—sweet tulip of Amarillo—um—I'll be coming for you—um—please be stillo! Oh, Cineverse! Why can't I remember any of these?"

Roger smiled as he pulled his horse up next to Louie and Lightning. But his grin vanished as he looked ahead. Where Doc and the cavalry had sung but a moment before, there was now nothing but a cloud of dust. Roger and Louie were all alone.

CHAPTER

⌒ **12** ⌒

"Now we've done it!" Big Louie moaned.

"Done what?" Roger asked. "What can happen to us in the middle of the desert?"

Louie mopped his brow with his neckerchief. "You mean, besides becoming victims of the elements, with no food or water, baked during the day and frozen at night, at the mercy of the desert sands?"

Roger admitted Louie had a point.

"And that's not the worst of it!" the small man continued. "What happens if Doctor Dread figures we're alone and comes back to get us?"

Roger sighed. If there was one problem with Louie, it was his slight tendency to get hysterical. "Doctor Dread has just escaped to some other place—some place in a Cineverse so vast we can't even begin to guess where it is," he replied evenly. "Why would he want to come back after us?"

Louie's gaze was still rather panic-stricken. He made a small mewling sound in the back of his throat.

Roger decided he'd try again. He calmly waved at his

surroundings. "Besides, this isn't as bad as all that, is it? We sang ourselves out here only a few hours ago. If Doc can sing them back to Sagebrush, why can't I do the same for us?"

"Oh, yeah?" Louie laughed hysterically. "Where do you think Doc got the guitar?"

Roger looked back at his now empty saddlebags.

"He's got my guitar?" Roger hesitated, feeling a bit of Louie's panic himself. "Oh, dear. And does Movie Magic work—"

"If you don't have a guitar?" Louie shook his head as he finished Roger's sentence for him. "Unfortunately, it's one of the Laws of the West. You either need a guitar, or a full orchestra, or you're stuck riding all the way back."

"A full orchestra?" Roger asked incredulously.

But Louie only nodded complacently. "You'd be surprised how handy they are, especially when you're singing songs about lovely Spanish señoritas."

The small man frowned as he changed the subject.

"And you're wrong about Doctor Dread, too. He does have a reason to come back. You see, I can find him."

"Oh," Roger replied. Was this good news or bad news? Good, he guessed, because it gave him a destination in his quest to rescue Delores. Then again, what wasn't so good was that—if Doctor Dread knew he might be pursued— the villain or one of his assistants could show up at any minute to put Roger and Louie "out of the way," as the Doctor would put it.

Of course, Roger realized upon reflection, this whole train of thought could be nothing more than the result of Big Louie's paranoia.

"Uh-oh," Big Louie whispered.

There was a cloud of dust before them where there had been nothing but desert before.

Then again, Roger thought, this whole train of thought could be totally, even overwhelmingly *justified* paranoia.

He stared into the dissipating dust, expecting at any second to discern a tall, thin man decked in signature snakeskin. And, indeed, he spotted a lone figure, walking toward them through the murky yellow cloud. However, instead of shiny black or green, the man in the dust was wearing clothes much the same color as the dirt that surrounded him, clothes that looked like they had been slept in for at least a month.

It wasn't Dread. It was Doc. And he was carrying a guitar.

"Shucks!" Doc drawled. "I thought you fellas were taggin' along. But when we got to Sagebrush, we discovered we were two hombres short." He nodded to Big Louie. "No offense."

Louie assured him there was none taken.

"Well, we were," Roger agreed, "tagging along, that is."

"We just fell a little behind," Louie confessed.

"Well, if *you* can make small jokes too, I guess I won't worry," Doc remarked. "Anyway, it's time I talked to you."

Doc pushed his battered and dusty hat farther back on his head as he looked from Roger to Louie and back again.

"You fellas have made me look at things in a different light. Pitched gun battles in town, showdowns in alleyways, last-minute rescues at secret hideouts—why, it's right like old times. I mean, after seeing action like that, who wants to go back to being a town drunk? I tell you, boys, I've groveled by my last spittoon." He spat for emphasis. "It was time to reexplore the hero business—but to do that, I had to talk to you. And you weren't there!"

He patted the wooden instrument at his side. "There was nothing left for me to do but pick up this old guitar and sing myself back your way."

"Gee," Roger said, quite overwhelmed by Doc's confession of faith.

"I tell you, those showdowns, gun battles, and rescues get in your blood," Doc continued nostalgically. "Reminds me of the way things used to be. So, I'd like to hitch up with you fellows." He paused, tugging his hat back down over his forehead. "That is, I would if you'd like a side-kick."

"Can a couple of sidekicks have a sidekick?" Louie grimaced. "I don't know. That sort of thing sounds to me like the Change coming back."

"No," Roger insisted. "This is no time to be fatalistic. Doc wants to leave the town-drunk business behind for a life of adventure, and I, for one, congratulate him! Besides, who knows? If the Change comes back, well, who says we can't work on it a little bit, and maybe it'll change our way?"

"Wow!" Louie replied in awe. "That's not a sidekick speech!"

"Land o' Goshen!" Doc echoed. "That sounds like hero talk to me!"

Well, Roger decided, he shouldn't let all this enthusiasm go to waste. He set his jaw in what he hoped was a grim and determined line, and said, with as much force as he could muster:

"Then it's time to find Dread and rescue the girl."

"Sounds right proper." Doc strummed meaningfully on his guitar. "Just let me know where, and I'll sing you there straightaway!"

"It's not as simple as that," Louie replied grimly. "Doctor Dread is not on this world."

"Not on this world?" Doc asked as he looked down at his guitar in dismay. "Then how can we possibly find him?"

"No problem," Louie assured the newest sidekick. "At least not with Roger here."

"Roger? Do you mean?" Doc asked with a touch of awe. "Does he have a ring?"

"He doesn't have a ring," Louie said proudly. "He doesn't need a ring. He has *methods*."

"*Methods?*" Doc parroted, his voice quivering with respect. "He calls himself a sidekick when he's got *methods*?"

"Oh, yeah," Roger replied rather quietly. "Well, I guess it's time to get those methods."

Roger realized that meant they had to use the ring. He unzipped the breast pocket of his running jacket and reached inside past the Mastercard, pulling out the round, gray key to the Cineverse.

"Here they are," Roger replied with a slightly embarrassed smile. "My methods."

"Hey!" Louie exclaimed. "I thought you said you didn't have a ring!"

Roger sighed. How could he explain this? He decided he couldn't.

"I was fibbing."

"Fibbing?" Doc squinted as he regarded Roger, his eyes no more than narrow but highly judgmental slits. "Maybe you're only a sidekick after all."

"I never claimed anything else," Roger said, hoping to calm the situation.

But Louie would not be calmed. He stuck a pudgy finger in Roger's face. "Hey! You told me you didn't have a ring. Were you hiding the ring from me?"

"Well, yes," Roger admitted.

"He hid the ring?" Doc's eyes were so narrow they were almost closed. "Sounds less like a hero with every minute."

"After all we've been through, you hid the ring?" Louie's hysteria seemed to be returning.

Roger did his best to keep his reply as calm as possible. "With all due respect, Louie, you used to be a bad guy."

"Oh, that," Louie replied in a much quieter tone. "I keep forgetting about that. I suppose you do have a point."

"You were a bad guy?" Doc asked, his eyes once again wide with wonder. "Then *you* must be the hero around here."

"Wait a moment," Roger said, once again feeling the logic of this place eluding him. "What do you mean by that?"

Doc nodded solemnly. "Reformed bad guys make some

of the best heroes. It's one of the Laws of the West."

"No, I'm no hero," Louie replied morosely. "I wasn't a very good bad guy, either. I simply have to face up to it: I was born a sidekick, and I'll be a sidekick till the day I die. Besides, I can't shoot a gun anywhere near as good as you." He nodded at Doc. "If there's a hero around here—"

"Denial?" Doc asked thoughtfully. "Humility? Heroic traits if I ever heard them."

"Listen," Roger insisted. "We don't have time to argue about who's the hero around here. We have a woman to rescue, and an evil genius to foil!"

"Then again," Doc added, "that decisiveness sounds pretty heroic to me, too."

"So we're all heroes!" Roger barked. "Well, at least we're heroic sidekicks. But we have things to do here!"

"He's the hero," Doc decided.

"Definitely," Louie agreed.

"Good to have that out of the way," Doc replied.

"It's a big load off my mind," Louie admitted.

"Can we get to work?" Roger demanded, holding out the ring. "We have places to go! How the heck do you use this ring?"

"He's the hero?" Doc asked.

"And he doesn't know how to use the ring?" Louie added.

"Well, I sort of do," Roger replied defensively. Actually, he hadn't wanted to admit his total ignorance of the ring's workings, but the way his two fellow sidekicks were going on and on had unnerved him, reminding him far too clearly of his public relations past and some committees he had been on for ever and ever. "After all," he added, "I got here, didn't I?"

"Maybe he's being humble now," Louie suggested. "Perhaps we should wait before we jump to conclusions here."

"True, true," Doc ruminated. "Heroing can be a subtle business sometimes."

"But I have no idea where we're going!" Roger shouted

at the conferees. "How can we rescue anybody when I don't know the destination!"

"Getting forceful again," Louie said approvingly.

Doc smiled. "I think I'm comfortable to leave him as the hero."

"Then it's agreed?" Louie asked.

The two shook hands.

Roger's patience was at an end.

"You!" He grabbed Louie by his red bandanna. "You know where Dread is hiding!"

"Then again," Louie rasped, "heroes seldom let their temper get the better of them."

"There's no such rule for sidekicks, is there?" Roger replied between clenched teeth.

"No, no," Louie managed. "Certainly not. In fact, there are many situations where the sidekick is required to get upset. It gives the hero somebody to calm down."

"Well, as soon as we find a hero, you'll be amazed how calm I'll get. But I don't think we're going to find anything unless we get out of here!"

Roger let go of Louie's neckerchief. The small man stepped back, massaging his neck. "Whoa! I didn't know you had that in you."

"You know," Doc mused, "he could be the antihero. Sometimes they lose—"

"Where are we going?" Roger screamed at Louie. "Now!"

"Oh, okay," Louie answered rapidly. "Turn the dial of the ring halfway around—"

"It's about time! Get off that horse!"

"What? Oh—um—okay." Totally flabbergasted, Louie did as he was told. Roger dismounted as well, and took a moment to change back into his more comfortable jogging suit. It was a relief not to have the silver Cavendish belt buckle digging into his stomach anymore.

"Now!" Roger twisted the ring, then grabbed the shoulders of his two companions. "See you in the funny papers!"

"No!" Louie cried as the three were surrounded by blue smoke. "Wait!"

But Roger was through with waiting. If Doc and Louie had had their way, they would have discussed the fine points of heroing until both Delores and the Cineverse were lost forever to the evil machinations of Doctor Dread. Sure, he'd had to be a little rough on them to get them to act. But it was the only way anything was going to happen. Roger felt fully justified in everything he'd had to do.

At least he did until the smoke cleared.

CHAPTER 13

"Duck!" Big Louie screamed.

Something exploded all too close. Roger, Doc, and Louie all hit the dirt. Louie pointed to a ditch behind them. Roger and the others crawled there as quickly as they could.

"A moment later, a grenade rolled against the small hill on which they had first appeared. A few seconds after that, the hill ceased to exist.

"Where are we?" Roger yelled at Louie, straining his voice to be heard over the screams and machine-gun fire.

"Darned if I know!" Louie yelled back.

"But didn't you tell me to turn the ring—"

"I told you to start by turning the ring!" The hysteria was back in Louie's voice. "I didn't tell you to finish off that way!"

A shell screamed over their heads. It hit a somewhat larger hill behind them, showering them with dirt and small rocks.

"This isn't where we're supposed to be?" Roger asked less calmly than he might have liked.

"Are you kidding?" Louie's laughter had a manic edge. "Would anybody choose to show up someplace like this?" A tank clanked angrily across the field before them. "I mean, how could something like this get any worse?"

"Uh, pardners?" Doc drawled. "Don't look now, but we've got company."

A man in green fatigues, a set of sergeant's stripes on his helmet, plopped down beside them in the ditch.

"Glad to see you guys finally got here," he began, but stopped when he got a closer look at the three of them. "How come you're out of uniform?"

"Uniform?" Roger asked before he could stop himself.

But Louie's explanation quickly followed: "We're supposed to penetrate enemy lines."

"Dressed like that?" the sergeant demanded. "You guys look like cowboys!" He pointed a thumb at Roger's shiny blue jogging suit. "Except for this one. He looks like a Martian!"

"Exactly," Louie explained without missing a beat. "It's psychological warfare."

"Really?" The sergeant scratched under his helmet. "Well, it had me fooled. Psychological warfare, you say? Gee. Maybe HQ actually got a good idea for a change."

The machine-gun fire redoubled above them, followed by shouts and screams of pain.

"Well, it's been awful nice chewing the fat with you," Louie remarked casually to the sergeant, "but we have a mission."

Roger stared at his fellow sidekick. Was Big Louie suggesting they leave their ditch to go out in that war up there? Sure, maybe Roger had gotten them into this in the first place by using the ring incorrectly. But there must be an easier way to get out of this than running through enemy fire.

"Your mission is canceled," the sergeant replied grimly. "I'm afraid your orders have been changed."

"Changed?" Louie demanded, indignant at the very thought.

Roger breathed a sigh of relief. Maybe he'd survive this mistake after all.

"That's right," the sergeant continued. "We need you three for a suicide mission."

"Suicide—" Roger began, his relief evaporating.

"Good of you to volunteer," the sergeant replied. "That's right, men. You've got to take Wishbone Hill!"

"Wishbone Hill?" Roger asked before he could stop himself.

"Glad to hear your enthusiasm," the sergeant answered. "Wishbone Hill. It's the reason we're all here, and the reason some of us will never leave. Sure, I know we've taken it twelve times already, and the enemy has captured it back as many times themselves. And every time, we've lost lives—good boys with homes and wives and mothers and fathers, boys just like you. But still we stay, and still we take that hill. Some might call it purposeless. Some might even call it crazy, a waste of human life. But we have to fight for what we believe in! There might be other battles in this war, but here we've got only one, and its name is Wishbone Hill. And now it's your job to take it!" He raised both fists in the air as he stared patriotically at his new recruits. "We can't let all those other boys die in vain! Do it for Bob! Do it for Artie!"

"Who's Bob?" Roger asked despite himself. "Who's Artie?"

"That's the spirit!" The sergeant gave Roger a hearty pat on the back. "Now get up that hill! After you're gone, we'll remember you, just like the others who have gone before, who gave their lives for the cause!"

"But, uh, we're not—" Roger tried again.

"Oh, it's natural to have a doubt or two." The sergeant chuckled ruefully. "Sure, maybe you're just tiny, meaningless cogs ground up in a giant war machine. And maybe that hill is no more than a pile of dirt that sooner or later will get blown away by the wind and the rain. But soon that won't matter to you anymore. When you make that hopeless charge up your final objective, wildly outnumbered by enemy firepower, cut down by flying bullets and shrapnel, the life's blood flowing from your body, you'll die happy, knowing you took that hill, and that we'll remember you, and call your names the next time we have to take it, and every time we take it after that!"

"Okay, Sarge," Louie announced before Roger could voice any further objections. "We'll take it!" He walked farther down the ditch, waving for Doc and Roger to follow.

"Wow, pardners," Doc whispered in wonder. "When I came with you looking for adventure, I never expected anything like this. Are you guys sure you're both sidekicks?"

"Soon to be dead sidekicks!" Roger's outburst was both hushed and vehement. "Are you crazy? We're probably going to get killed out there!"

"It's worse than that," Louie whispered back. "I'm from Brooklyn."

"So?" Roger asked, sure he was missing something again.

"If I go out there," Louie explained, "there's no 'probably' about it. The guy from Brooklyn always buys it in these plots."

"A Law of the West?" Roger asked.

"We're no longer in the West," Louie reminded him. "In a place like this, I think you call it a Rule of Battle."

"Yeah," Doc drawled, "or maybe the Fortunes of War."

Roger still didn't understand. "So why did you tell that guy we'd do it?"

"To give you a chance to use that ring of yours," Louie explained.

"I can't use it in the ditch?"

"You can't use it around the sergeant. If you do, bad things might happen. In a way, it's sort of a Cineverse courtesy—you keep the ring as far away from the current plot line as possible. It's rumored that doing it any other way promotes the Change."

Roger guessed that made sense. Both the worlds he had visited in the Cineverse seemed to have a central plot line —in the West, it was getting the Cavendishes; here, it was taking Wishbone Hill—and those plot lines could be disrupted by outside forces, especially if that force was as powerful as the Captain Crusader Decoder Ring.

"So we have to get away from the sergeant?" he asked.

Louie nodded.

Roger didn't like the direction Louie's logic was taking. "And there's only one way to do that?"

Louie nodded again.

Roger supposed there was no helping it. "Up the hill?"

"Towards the hill," Louie amended. "But not very far."

Louie explained his plan.

"You mean we're not going to take Wishbone Hill?" Doc asked in disappointment.

"Trust me," Louie replied. "We'll have other adventures. Some we might even live through."

"Well, all right," Doc said reluctantly. "'Though I was looking forward to taking out some of those machine guns with my six-shooter. Still, if you promise there'll be more excitement—"

"Trust me," Louie repeated. "I don't think there's any way we can get away from the excitement."

It sounded good to Doc. It didn't sound so good to Roger, but he'd vowed he'd go through anything, even excitement, to rescue Delores. This time, he carefully followed Louie's instructions for setting the ring.

"Well?" the sergeant called impatiently from the other end of the ditch.

"Right, Sarge!" Louie called back. "It's time, men. Over the top."

Roger reset his ring and the three men joined hands as they leapt from the ditch, immediately falling to their hands and knees as they screamed in unison:

"See you in the funny papers!"

"Avast!"

The blue smoke was clearing quickly, blown away by a sea breeze.

"Witchcraft!"

Roger let go of his two cronies and looked up from

his kneeling position. They seemed to be on a boat—a three-masted schooner was Roger's guess. There also seemed to be a swordfight going on—or at least there had been until Roger and his fellow sidekicks had interrupted the proceedings.

Louie grinned and waved. "Excuse us, folks. Just passing through."

"Aha, fiends!" a fellow with an eye patch replied as he brandished his sword. "See how you laugh after you've tasted naked steel!"

"We'd rather not, thank you," Roger answered respectfully.

But politeness didn't seem to be working. A dozen sword-wielding men, some in uniform, others dressed in colorful rags, advanced upon them.

"What say we split his gizzard?" Eye Patch asked no one in particular.

"Is this where we're supposed to be?" Roger whispered to Louie. Roger didn't even know where his gizzard was, but he wasn't too anxious to find out.

"I don't think so," Louie whispered back. He flinched as Eye Patch brandished his sword in their general direction.

"But you had me twist the ring—"

Louie frowned, his eyes darting back and forth between a dozen swords. "It would have worked if you hadn't jumped the gun and landed us in the middle of a war zone. And now this!" He leapt back, even though the nearest sword was still a good six feet away. "From here on in, setting the ring is going to involve a certain amount of guesswork—at least until we end up someplace that I recognize. The Captain Crusader Decoder Ring is a delicate instrument. It also doesn't help that it's very cheaply made, and almost impossible to turn."

"Oh," Roger replied. He had thought it was his inexperience that was making it difficult to use the ring. Somehow, he found that thought preferable to the idea that the key to the Cineverse could fall apart at any minute.

"Let's split all their gizzards!" Eye Patch announced

with a chuckle. The eleven men behind him brandished their swords in unison.

"I think it's time for some fancy shootin'," Doc announced, starting to rise. A couple of the colorfully garbed fellows drew flintlock pistols from their waistbands. They obviously thought shooting was a good idea, too.

"No it isn't," Louie announced. "It's time to get out of here, now!" He grabbed Roger's ring hand and Doc's pant leg, shouting:

"See you in the funny papers!"

The blue smoke swallowed them.

Roger heard metal clang against metal, the unmistakable sound of dueling swords!

"Uh-oh," Louie whispered.

The blue smoke was still thick around them. A clipped British accent cursed the deuced fog.

"What do you mean, uh-oh?" Roger asked.

"I panicked back there," was Louie's only explanation.

"Yep," Doc agreed. "We sure skedaddled out of that place."

Even more clipped British accents began to swear in their vicinity.

"So?" Roger asked, still not quite comprehending their danger.

On the other hand, as the swearing increased, the sword fight sounds had ceased entirely.

"You remember what I said about plot lines?" Louie explained. "I not only panicked—I may have panicked too close to the middle of one of them."

"I say!" one of the local voices interjected. "There are intruders in our midst!"

Had they been discovered? Roger waited a moment for something to happen. Nothing did. The blue smoke seemed to be hanging around for an awfully long time on this go-round.

"And?" Roger finally prompted when Big Louie gave no further explanation. It had something to do with the swords, didn't it? "You mean, we haven't left the pirate world?"

"It's more of the robbers!" shouted one of the voices out there in the smoke.

"Well, no, we're probably not there anymore—" Big Louie began without much enthusiasm.

"Nonsense!" another fog voice interjected. "It's the duke's men!"

"But we haven't gotten very far," Louie continued morosely. "Maybe it's nothing to worry about. It hardly ever happens—it's just something you hear about, mostly—but when you do fall into one, you're really in trouble."

Roger could see sunlight overhead. The blue fog was finally starting to dissipate. Any number of sword fights resumed. The clanging and grunting was everywhere. There seemed to be a dozen pitched battles all around them.

"Sounds to me," Doc cracked, "like the adventure's just beginnin'."

The smoke cleared at last.

If anything, Roger decided Doc had underestimated the situation.

CHAPTER

⟁ 14 ⟁

"Oh, dear," Louie moaned.

Now that the smoke was gone, Roger could see that they were in the middle of a crowd—a very active crowd.

First off, there were two distinct groups of men fighting each other with swords. One group was dressed in bright but motley clothes of more-or-less forest green. They leapt and capered about as they fought, exchanging witticisms with their fellows and laughing cheerily as they impaled members of the other group on their flashing blades.

"But if that's true," Louie said, more to himself than the others, "what can we do?" He stared morosely at the Captain Crusader Decoder Ring in Roger's hand.

Roger hauled Big Louie back a step as the fight surged in their direction. The small sidekick seemed too entangled in their own dilemma to worry about anything as minor as a nearby sword fight. Roger scanned the surrounding crowd, hoping he might find somewhere they might be a little less exposed to the melee.

The foes of the men in green were a far more sober bunch. They were better dressed than the others, most of them wearing an embroidered red-and-white overshirt covering chain mail, with bullet-shaped helmets on their heads. They seemed to be decent enough swordsmen, although they showed none of the flair of their green-suited adversaries, and the chain mail seemed to be no protection at all from enemy swords.

At first glance, backed by years of movie-viewing experience, Roger surmised that the folks in green were the "robbers," while the bullet helmets were the "duke's men." There were others around as well, townspeople dressed mostly in the drabbest of browns, and a young woman, who, by her extremely fine and colorful dress, he assumed was of the nobility—a dark-haired woman who was almost as attractive as Delores.

Delores! Images of blond hair and dazzling smiles were pushed aside by the laughter of Doctor Dread. No, Roger told himself, no matter how difficult, he had to figure out how to get out of his present situation before he could rescue the woman in his life.

That is, if he could even figure out this particular situation—especially whatever it was that Louie was muttering so darkly about.

Actually, those things going on immediately in front of him were easy to comprehend. While he had never been so close to one of those sword fights before, he had certainly witnessed this kind of scene a thousand times on a movie screen. Why, it only took him a moment, glancing around at the jumping bodies and clashing swords, to determine the star players in this little drama.

A tall and thin yet muscular fellow, dressed in a slightly brighter shade of green than his fellows, faced off against another of the chain-mailed band, this one sporting a much larger white fleur-de-lis on his red shirt than his compatriots. The chain-mailed man moved well with a sword, too, if a bit too fussily. He was also tall and slender, but to almost too great a degree, as if he were perhaps the product of a bit too much royal inbreeding.

"Take that, you cur!" the leader of the duke's men called.

His opponent smiled dashingly.

"You call me a cur, sir," he replied as he pressed his attack. "Well, perhaps I am, if you define a cur as a man who loves freedom!"

The freedom-lover easily repelled a new attack by the duke's man with three quick flicks of his sword. The duke's lackey took a step away to catch his breath and wipe the sweat from his brow. The freedom-lover paused as well, amused by his opponent's lack of stamina. Despite the rags, you could tell who the true nobleman was around here.

"Wait until the duke hears about this," the duke's man wheezed, "you scoundrel!"

The freedom-lover raised a single, handsome eyebrow. "Scoundrel? Well, perhaps I am, Sheriff, if scoundrels defend the rights of common people!"

The townspeople cheered. The sheriff could clearly see the tide of events turning against him.

Louie turned to Roger, grabbing the front of his jogging suit with panicked hands.

"We've got to get out of here!" he whispered hoarsely.

"And don't think, Sheriff," the freedom-lover continued smoothly, "that I haven't noticed your new recruits!" With a grin, he waved at Roger and his fellows.

"Too late," Louie moaned.

"My recruits?" The sheriff barked an affected laugh. "Who are these people?" He glanced disdainfully at Roger's band. "Surely they are dressed as traveling minstrels—no, no, traveling minstrels would have more taste! No—" He paused to sneer. "They are dressed even worse than the men of the forest—more like clowns!"

Clowns? Roger wondered if that was a demotion from sidekick.

"Clowns?" That last reference was too much for the freedom-lover to take. Once again he pressed his attack. "Well, perhaps we are, if a clown is anyone who laughs at oppression!"

His sword thrust was desperately parried at the last possible moment by the sheriff.

"The duke's will shall not be mocked!" the sheriff insisted hysterically. He waved his free hand in Roger's general direction. "Men! Let's give these three interlopers a taste of naked steel!"

Louie whimpered.

"Don't listen to them, free men of the forest!" the green-clad leader replied. "These three clown-garbed newcomers are obviously one of the duke's tricks! Dispense with them, as you would with all men who would usurp the true heir to the throne! If they shall taste naked steel, it will be the naked steel of justice!"

Men in green rushed Roger and his company from one side, men in helmets from the other. All of them appeared to have very sharp swords.

"I can't help myself!" Louie wailed. He snatched the ring out of Roger's hand.

They were surrounded by blue smoke.

"I'm sorry," Louie muttered through the smoke. "I'm really sorry."

"Is our little buddy always this cheerful?" Doc inquired.

"I've always had this thing about—swords," Louie confessed.

Roger tried to be the voice of reason. "But there aren't any swords out there now!" All sounds of battle had vanished with the last use of the ring. Roger could hear nothing now but the distant sound of the sea.

"Especially swords pointed at me," Louie continued hastily, as if his fear were a demon he had to exorcise.

"There were hardly ever any swords in comedy relief. Oh, why—"

A door opened somewhere. Louie's voice died as the smoke cleared.

"And who invades the chambers of Bonnie Kate, Queen of the Swordswomen?"

A tall, handsome woman menaced them with a sword.

"Perhaps you shall answer some questions," she remarked with a sardonic grin, "when you are confronted by naked steel?"

Louie screamed.

They were surrounded by blue smoke.

"I've done it now," Louie groaned.

"What?" Roger couldn't handle this anymore. "What have you done?" he demanded.

"Doomed us all," Louie answered.

Roger had to admit it—he was getting tired of this small fellow's negative attitude. Even more than that, he was getting tired of all this blue smoke. It seemed to get worse with every new movie world they traveled to.

"You've noticed how bad the smoke is getting," Louie echoed, even though Roger hadn't voiced his thoughts aloud. Louie sighed heavily. "That's another sign."

"You say you were in comedy relief?" Doc drawled. "Are you sure you weren't asked to leave?"

Louie ignored the questions, preferring instead to work himself into a moderate state of hysteria. "Oh, if only I knew more about how this cheap plastic ring really worked! I've only heard the rumors—old wives' tales, I thought until now! Hah!"

Roger tried to face Louie in the blue fog.

What rumors? he yelled at the top of his voice.

"If something happens to your ring," Louie explained at last, "or if you use it too close to a world's central plot line, you can be trapped."

"Trapped?" Roger asked. "How?"

"You've seen it—haven't you? First, we were surrounded by pirates, then we ended up in the middle of some sort of noble-outlaws versus the-corrupt-authorities thing, and we get out of that, only to be confronted by the Queen of the Swordswomen!"

Roger could see his point. There was a certain similarity here.

"They're all swashbucklers," he said aloud.

"I've trapped us in a movie cycle," Louie whispered. "We may have to spend the rest of our lives—admittedly short ones—threatened, over and over again, by naked steel!"

"Now, now." Roger spoke reassuringly, trying to calm the small man down. "We don't know that we're trapped anywhere in particular. You said yourself that using the ring would be a matter of trial and error until we found some territory that we were familiar with. The fact that we've visited three similar movie worlds in a row might simply be—coincidence."

There, that sounded at least moderately convincing. Roger wished he could believe it himself.

"So—we might be somewhere else when this blue smoke finally clears?" Louie asked, only half-doubtfully. Against all reason, it seemed he wanted to believe Roger's theory. "If only it could be so!"

As if on cue, the blue smoke evaporated around them. They stood on a dock, in a sun-filled seaport, with a full-rigged sailing ship before them.

"But I don't think it is," Louie moaned.

Doc nodded in commiseration. "I reckon we're back with the pirates."

"Not necessarily!" Roger insisted, trying somehow not to give into despair. He couldn't help himself. There was no such word as despair in public relations.

"Pirates?" A nearby fellow shouted at them as he hobbled forward on his wooden peg leg. He wore a three-cornered hat, and sported a multicolored parrot on his shoulder. Roger had to admit, it certainly looked like pirates.

"No pirates around here!" Peg Leg announced, contradicting his appearance. "We and my mates are buccaneers!"

"Squawk!" the parrot agreed. "Happy buccaneers!"

"All my fault," Louie muttered. "If only I didn't have this thing about swords."

"Isn't that right, mates?" Peg Leg called.

"Aye!" fifty-odd cheerful voices called from the nearby ship.

"And how do we prove to these strangers here—"

"Squawk!" the parrot interrupted. "Happy strangers!"

"That we're happy buccaneers?" Peg Leg finished.

Roger half expected the answer to be naked steel.

Instead, the fifty-odd sailors shouted back:

"With a happy song!"

Louie, if possible, became even more ashen-faced than before.

"Oh, no," he breathed. "Not a singing swashbuckler!"

"Squawk!" the parrot agreed. "Happy singing swashbuckler!"

And fifty-odd manly voices broke out in song:

"Oh, we sail all the seven seas,
    Rob Spanish galleons as we please;
    But honest men will have no fear
    Of the happy singing buccaneers!"

Louie looked up at Roger. "I knew it would be bad. I didn't know it would be this bad."

"Now," Doc observed, "this doesn't seem much different from a singing Western." He pulled the guitar around from where he had been carrying it on his back. He strummed a few experimental chords. "Just give me a couple moments, and we could do right well in these here parts."

"Perhaps you are right." Big Louie shivered. "It could be even worse. There are still more dangerous worlds than this—worlds where music is even more in evidence!"

Louie paused for an instant, frozen, when he saw some of the buccaneers were happily waving swords.

"But," he forced himself to continue at last, "it makes no difference. When you're trapped, how can anything make a difference?"

"Trapped?" Roger asked, still needing to be convinced. "But how do you know that? We have been going from swashbuckler to swashbuckler, that is true, but one was on sea, the next on land, the third featured a female protagonist, and the fourth seems to be full of comedy and song. We should be near the cycle's end, shouldn't we?"

"Cycles never end in the Cineverse," Louie disagreed. "Besides, there's something more. You see, there's one problem I haven't told you about."

Louie was interrupted by the buccaneers' second verse:

> "We rob, we loot, we pillage, too,
>   And we'll sing a song for you!
>   We use our swords in all good cheer;
>   We're the happy, singing buccaneers!"

Louie stared blankly out at the tuneful shipmates.

"One problem?" Roger reminded him.

He blinked and turned back to Roger. "How do I say this?" he began in a voice that suggested he himself didn't believe what he was talking about. "The last time the blue smoke showed up—I hadn't even touched the ring."

Doc stared at the sidekick. "You mean the blue smoke got the notion to show up by itself?"

Louie nodded as he fearfully blurted words that he did not want to speak. "What have I done? In my haste to get away from a sword, I may have—unsettled the very fabric of the Cineverse!"

Before Roger could think of anything to say, the shipmates had launched into their third verse:

"We're happy, singing buccaneers,
And all our friends need never fear,
But all opposed will surely feel,
A brace of cannon and naked steel!"

Louie screamed. The blue smoke wasn't far behind.

And this time, Roger had seen, Louie had done nothing at all with the ring.

Even with his public relations training, he had to admit it. This time, it looked like they were in real trouble.

CHAPTER
15

The tone of the next voice they heard through the blue smoke was distressingly familiar.

"Avast! What did I tell you, me hearties! You don't get away from Captain Wishbone that easily!"

"*Now* we're back with the pirates," Louie remarked fatalistically.

"Aye, mateys!" the captain's voice continued jovially. "It looks like gizzard-splitting time is here after all!"

So it was a cycle after all, Roger thought—an apparently unbroken cycle. Well, Louie may have been ready to give up on their chances of survival, but Roger wasn't. He felt you could deal with any situation, once you understood it.

It was the understanding part that got difficult around here. Still, Roger was ready to try. Maybe there was some way to reason with the denizens of this particular movie world, find out how they fit into the cycle, even define the limits of the cycle itself. Louie may have made a mistake, but Roger didn't yet think that mistake was fatal.

When the smoke cleared, Roger saw that the twelve

pirates had formed a circle around them. Their swords were drawn, their eyes filled with menace. Roger realized there was more than one way for things to be fatal in this situation.

He cleared his throat.

"Pardon me. Can we talk?"

The pirates all laughed.

"You're talkin' now, aren't ya?" one particularly grizzled specimen replied colorfully, "Sure. We always lets 'em talk, 'afore we splits 'eir gizzards!"

"Oh," Roger replied, afraid he had understood all too much of the pirate's colorful dialect. "But is gizzard-splitting entirely necessary?"

"'E mought 'ave a point 'ere, Cap'n!" the grizzled fellow remarked with a gap-toothed grin.

"Aye," another member of the crew piped up. "We could keelhaul them instead!"

"There's always the cat-o'-nine-tails—" yet another crew member began helpfully.

"Not dramatic enough!" a fourth pirate insisted. "Let's do this proper. Drawing and quartering!"

"But a flogging!" the cat-o'-nine-tails crew member insisted. "It's been ever so long since we've had a good flogging!"

"'Ere noo, the grizzled fellow interrupted with a sprightly wink of his good eye. "Wot aboot 'e traditional values?"

Roger managed to take a breath. At least someone here was going to stand up for their rights!

A bearded gent with a three-cornered captain's hat grinned at the grizzled man. "What's that you say, Briny? Traditional values?"

"Aye, aye, Cap'n Wishbone," Briny replied as he colorfully coughed a wad of phlegm. "We shood mak'em walk 'e plank!"

Maybe, Roger considered, discussion wasn't the best course of action in their present situation.

Apparently, Doc felt the same way, for he had drawn both his six-shooters.

"Seems to me," he drawled, "that these fellows will show us a little more respect once they get a little ventilation."

Louie plucked at Doc's dusty sleeve.

"It won't work."

"What do you mean, it won't work?" Doc took careful aim at the captain. "Western justice always works!"

"In the West," Louie reminded him

Doc pulled twin triggers. Nothing happened.

"It's Movie Magic," Louie explained. "It can work against you, too. Your six-guns can't possibly shoot here. They haven't been invented yet."

The pirates, who had hung back for a moment when Doc had drawn his guns, all decided they had had enough talk.

"Hells bells!" the captain intoned. "Why do we have to kill these fellows only one way?"

"You mean we could flog them—" the cat-o'-nine-tails enthusiast began.

"And then we could keelhaul them?" another added.

"An' den we can split 'eir gizzards, draw an' quarter 'em, an' make 'em walk 'e plank!" Briny added, getting into the spirit of things.

The pirates all liked that plan a lot. They pushed their swords toward Roger, Louie, and Doc.

"There's only one thing to do," Louie replied miserably. He screamed, and the blue smoke was back.

At least, Roger thought, no one had mentioned naked steel.

"'Tis the duke's lackeys, skulking amongst us once again!" a voice yelled.

"Nonsense!" a second voice replied. "Pay no attention to this forest-bred trick!"

Roger thought quickly, knowing he had a moment to spare before the ever-more-sluggish blue smoke cleared. Perhaps it had been foolish to even try to reason with the band of pirates—by definition, they were all bad guys, after all. Here though, in the world of the duke and the forest, there were two rival factions, one of which had to be the good guys—by default, if for no other reason. And, by the very laws of movie logic, where there were good guys, there had to be somebody he could reason with.

He remembered the bold man in green, and the overly fussy sheriff. He could guess who the hero was around here, but he might—conceivably—be wrong. He had already made a mistake or two since he had entered the Cineverse, after all. He would simply have to present his case, see how the two factions reacted, and act accordingly.

He had made his decision.

"Let me handle this," he whispered to Louie and Doc. "I have a plan."

Obligingly, the blue smoke cleared in that instant.

"Royal lackeys!" the men in green called.

"Forest swine!" the bullet helmets shot back.

Roger held up his hands for silence. Surprisingly enough, he got it. Now all he had to do was present his case convincingly enough so that he might come under the protection of one side or the other—a protection that would give him and his fellows time to see if there was an alternative to being trapped in this cycle.

But how should he begin? He had tried once before—on the Western world—to win over the confidence of the locals, with somewhat less than perfect results. He would simply have to do better here.

"Good men of this kingdom!" he began. That sounded neutral enough, and, indeed, neither side seemed particularly upset to be addressed in that manner.

"We fight for neither the duke nor the forest!" he continued, adding quickly: "Not that your cause is not just—" He was careful not to mention which cause. "For we are new in this part of the world, and woefully ignorant of the outrages that have been visited upon you." He figured that line was pretty safe—both sides appeared reasonably outraged. And, as he took a pause for breath, he noticed that both sides had begun to mutter darkly as they glared at each other from opposite sides of the marketplace.

"However," he went on before it could become more

than muttering, "if you would be willing to speak with us but for a moment, I am sure we would quickly see the justice—"

Both sides began to shout before he could get any further.

"Any true son of the kingdom would see how the duke has abused—" the leader of the men in green shouted.

"Any true son of the kingdom would be loyal to the Duke of Wishbone—" the sheriff insisted.

Oh, dear. Roger didn't want this to get out of hand.

"Good people," he began before he got outshouted again.

"Loyal to the duke?" The green leader laughed. "Who stole the throne from the rightful heir—"

"Would you listen to these men?" the sheriff retorted. "Common thieves, who must hide in the forest—"

"Is this part of your plan?" Louie whispered.

"And what of the time when good King Reg returns from the Crusades—?"

"King Reg? Don't make me laugh!" The sheriff laughed anyway. "He gave up that title when he went gallivanting off on his private errand!"

"Must be a pretty good plan." Doc whistled. "It's sure got me stumped."

"Oh, yes?" the sheriff's opponent demanded. "And what about the crown jewels?"

Roger had to admit that this particular exchange had him stumped, too. And it wasn't getting any of them any closer to escaping from this cycle.

"You cannot accuse us of that!" the sheriff replied vehemently. "Everyone knows the crown jewels fell into the hands of—"

"Enough!" Roger yelled. He didn't care the slightest bit whose hands the crown jewels had fallen into. All he wanted was some way out of here. If his plan was going to work, it was time to get tough.

"Where is the truth?" he demanded before the factions could resume their shouting contest. "How can we choose a side when you are reduced to petty bickering!"

"Bickering?" the leader in green demanded. "I suppose I am, if bickering is defending the rights of the downtrodden!"

"*Petty* bickering?" the sheriff echoed. "We'll show you what happens to those who call the duke's actions *petty*!"

"Uh, Roger?" Louie pulled on his sleeve. "This isn't the plan, is it?"

"Well, I can tell you one thing!" the man in green declared. "These newcomers are no part of the true men of the forest!"

"And they certainly do not have the best interests of the duke at heart!" the sheriff agreed.

"They must be agents of the queen—" another of the forest men shouted.

"No, no!" one of the duke's men countered. "They are most assuredly spies for the King of Spain!"

"There are certain ministers high in government who are known to have been plotting—" another forester mused.

"It's not that at all!" a fellow in a bullet helmet ventured. "There are elements in the Church who have been waiting years for just such an opportunity—"

Everyone turned to stare at Roger and his companions. There was a moment of awkward silence. This had not worked at all in the manner Roger had hoped. Maybe, he thought, if he started all over again—

"Good people of this kingdom—" he began.

Both groups groaned.

"We don't have to go through this again, do we?" the sheriff complained.

His opponent shook his head, a new determination upon his handsome features. "I say, let's kill them quickly, and get back to our fight."

"No," Louie moaned. "I don't think this was the plan."

"For once, outlaw," the sheriff answered the man in green, rewarding his opposite with a somewhat fussy smile, "we agree on something. Have at them, soldiers!"

The forest leader laughed, once again confident of his priorities. "Men! Skewer them with naked steel!"

Any number of men with swords rushed them again.

The blue smoke showed up before Louie could even whimper.

"All my fault," Louie muttered.

Even Roger was beginning to believe that Louie might be right. But, call him an optimistic fool who'd spent too long in public relations—or, for that matter, call him somebody who didn't even want to think about the consequences if they really were stuck here—whatever the reason, he wasn't quite ready to give up yet.

Louie misused the ring, and the ring malfunctioned. Louie still had the ring and the ring still malfunctioned. Even Roger could see there was a common thread here.

"Louie," he said calmly. "There's one other way we can try to stop this thing. Give me back the ring."

"Oh." Louie paused. "Do you think?"

Roger could hear the relief in Louie's voice. So even the sidekick thought it was a good idea!

"Sure," Louie agreed, "as soon as the smoke clears."

"Aye," a woman's voice came out of the fog. "We're waitin' for that, too."

"Uh-oh," Louie replied.

Roger knew exactly what the sidekick meant. It had to be Bonnie Kate, Queen of the Swordswomen! Well, maybe if he started talking while they were still lost in this impenetrable cloud, he'd have enough time to convince Kate that the three of them meant no harm.

"Might I speak with you?" Roger asked.

"You might as well," Kate replied sassily. "We can do nought else while we wait for this blue bedevilment to clear."

"You know we mean you no harm," Roger replied.

"So you say," Kate answered noncommittally.

"We need a place to rest," Roger added.

"I've heard that before," she answered with a laugh.

"Uh—" Roger answered. This didn't seem to be going any better than the last couple of times. Shouldn't he be getting better with experience?

"Excuse me for interruptin'," Doc drawled, "but this

wouldn't happen to be another one of your plans?"

"Well," Roger admitted, "I don't think I've quite gotten to the planning stage."

"Just wanted to be ready," Doc added amiably. "There's probably still some way out of this. You never know—six-guns might work here."

"Have you got a better idea?" Roger demanded.

"You're the hero around here," Doc deferred.

Not again, Roger thought.

"Who came up with that idea?" he insisted.

"We all did, remember?" Louie chimed in. "You were elected by popular vote."

Roger didn't recall it in exactly that way. Still, this probably wasn't the best time to argue the point.

"You were trying to convince us?" Kate's voice penetrated the blue fog.

Roger sighed. He shouldn't have to be reminded that he was in the middle of a speech, trying to save his own life and those of his companions, not to mention the entire fate of the Cineverse. Still, thanks to Kate's interjection, he was back on track now. It was time to get down to business.

"As I was saying," he continued into the blue smoke in what he hoped was Kate's general direction. "We are but three travelers, intent on harming no one, whose only wish is to find a quiet place that we might rest for a bit in order to better determine the best way that we might find our home."

That was the best explanation Roger could come up with. If that wouldn't work, he didn't know what would.

"You make such a pretty speech—" Kate began as the smoke finally cleared.

The dark-haired Kate was flanked by two other women —one blond, the other a redhead—both without a doubt members of Kate's all-woman crew. All three were dressed in pirate costumes of tight breeches and revealing vests.

"It's a shame we could never trust you!" Kate finished up as all three brandished their swords.

"What?" Roger asked, dumbfounded. "You mean you can't trust outsiders?"

Kate sneered at the suggestion. "Outsiders? We welcome outsiders! We've learned that you can't trust—men! What say, ladies? Let's gut them and throw them over the side to feed the fish!"

The blue smoke was back, all too soon.

Roger realized they were running out of options.

He hoped, somehow, they might be able to sing their way to safety.

In the meantime, he realized, Louie still hadn't given him the ring.

"Louie!" he yelled as they heard the first strains of cheerful song:

> "People quake when they see our boat!
>   We'll sing to you and cut your throat;
>   We'll take your nose as a souvenir;
>   We're happy, singing buccaneers!"

"The visitors are back!" somebody yelled in acknowledgment of the blue smoke.

"Squawk!" the parrot added. "Happy visitors!"

Obviously, Roger reflected, the parrot didn't know them very well.

"What's the matter?" Louie called back to Roger. "I mean, besides everything?"

"You haven't given me the ring!" Roger answered.

"Oh." Louie sighed. "We haven't stopped anywhere long enough for me to think about it."

"At this rate," Roger reminded him, "we may never have any time to stop anywhere again. I'm holding out my hand. You'll have to give me the ring before the smoke clears!"

"Is that a smart move?" Louie asked. "Passing the ring when we can't see it? We could lose it!"

"So?" Doc interjected. "The way things are going, losing the dang ring might be better for all of us!"

"Doc has a point," Roger admitted. "Give it here."

"See?" Louie said defensively. "You still talk like a hero."

Roger thought about objecting again, but what was the use? Besides, he felt something hard, round, and plastic being pressed into his palm. He closed his fingers around it. Now, maybe, something would happen!

There was a sound like thunder, so close that Roger jumped. The blue smoke disappeared, but it was replaced this time by blackness.

Perhaps, he thought belatedly, taking the ring wasn't such a good idea.

CHAPTER

⬥ 16 ⬥

Then the smoke returned, darker than before, now a true midnight-blue.

"Avast!" a gruff voice called. "The landlubbers are back, ready to walk the plank!"

"It's the pirate world!" Louie screamed.

Roger realized they must have jumped again when he got the ring.

"I say," another voice remarked, "don't those blighters know when to stop bothering the free men of the forest?"

"No, it's not!" Doc interjected. "It's the fellas with the funny helmets!"

"Cowards, all cowards!" a woman's voice called next. "Isn't that just like men?"

"No, it isn't!" Roger yelled in turn. "Can't you see? It's much worse than that!"

"We'll make a necklace of their ears," the male chorus interjected. "We're happy, singing buccaneers!"

"Something's happened with the ring," Roger explained. "Instead of slowing things down, when Louie gave me the ring, it stepped things up. We're going faster and faster, almost as if we were being sucked into some sort of Cineverse vortex!"

Doc whistled. "Sure sounds like a hero's explanation to me."

Roger tried to think what he could do. If only he understood the true workings of the Captain Crusader Decoder Ring—if only he understood anything about what had happened to him since Delores disappeared!

Delores!

No, he had to keep his wits. Things were still changing around him. Even though he couldn't see anything but the deep blue smoke, the voices around him seemed to be growing louder.

"Where did this—ship come from?" the leader of the forest men asked, his voice edged with hysteria. "Is this another one of the duke's tricks?"

"Aye, Cap'n," Briny's unmistakable slur cut in. "Look at 'ese wenches!"

"I'll wench you, you male rumbuckets!" Kate replied haughtily.

"Squawk!" the parrot added. "Happy rumbuckets!"

"Oh, no," Louie yelled in Roger's ear. "All the worlds are coming together! You know what that means, don't you?"

Roger had no idea.

"It's the Change!" Louie screamed. "We have to do something!"

"This is all some forest trick!" the sheriff yelled.

"As killers, we're the most sincere!" the male chorus warbled. "We're happy, singing—"

Roger felt someone grab his lapels.

"Roger!" Louie continued to yell in his ear. "Why didn't I think of this before? Quick! Before its too late! You have to use your methods!"

What? Roger thought. Methods? But hadn't he explained to Louie that his so-called methods were only a ruse, that he really never had any more than a Captain Crusader Decoder Ring?—a ring that he didn't know how to use very well.

"It's our only chance!" the sidekick pleaded.

Well, apparently Roger hadn't explained it well enough. Either Louie had misunderstood—or he had completely forgotten—Roger's explanation.

One more thing had become very apparent in their present crisis: Roger had always known that he understood very little of what was going on around him, but now he realized he didn't understand anything at all. He had no idea of what these so-called methods might be. Of course, he didn't think Louie or Doc had any more idea of what "methods" would be than he did.

He realized that might be the answer. One of the great underlying axioms of public relations was that you approached everything in the most positive manner possible. Perhaps he just had to approach these methods positively. If it would help to have Louie believe he had methods, let him believe it. And maybe, Roger realized, if he believed he had methods, he would have.

"All right," Roger replied reluctantly. "I'll use my methods if I have to."

"See?" Doc chortled. "A hero will always come through in the end!"

Roger wished he had Doc's confidence. In the meantime, though, he had to invent some methods.

"Listen to me," he yelled, "O Lords of the Cineverse!"

That sounded good, didn't it? But methods had to be more than that. Secret words, maybe?

"D. W. Griffith!" he yelled. "David O. Selznick! Cecil B. de Mille!"

Nothing but smoke. Maybe he should use the ring, too? Why not? It certainly couldn't get any worse than this.

Roger crossed his fingers as he twisted the ring.

"Get us out of here!" he yelled.

The blue smoke was gone, replaced again by the total absence of light. Uh-oh. Maybe it could get worse.

"Help!" he added.

And there was light. And there were voices singing. Not the male voices of the buccaneers, but a mixed chorus, with perhaps a bit heavier emphasis on the high, ethereal end of the vocal scale; a Mormon Tabernacle choir sort of feeling. Roger blinked, trying to adjust his eyes to the sudden illumination. Louie and Doc were still with him, one to either side. And there was someone else here, too—no, not the choir. Those voices seemed to come from everywhere as if from a host of invisible angels, or perhaps a really good sound system. But there was a tall figure, dressed all in white, who stood before that brilliant light, an illumination so intense that Roger could not really focus on the details of the figure.

And then the figure spoke:

LOUIE!

It was the loudest voice Roger had ever heard.

LONG TIME, NO SEE!

Louie only stood and stared. The voice boomed on:

FOOLISH OF ME.
YOU WOULDN'T REMEMBER, WOULD YOU?

Louie shook his head.

"It couldn't be," he whispered.

AND DOC.
YOU'RE LOOKING GOOD!

Doc nodded, pleasantly enough, Roger guessed, but he noticed the cowboy kept his hands close to his six-shooters.

WHO'S THIS NEW FELLOW?
DON'T TELL ME, I SHOULD KNOW.
ROGER, IS IT?
IT ALWAYS TAKES ME A MINUTE
WITH OUTSIDERS.

"It is," Louie whispered in awe. "It's the Plotmaster!"

Doc's hands left his gun handles as his mouth dropped open.

"Tarnation! The Plotmaster?"

Roger squinted over at the booming fellow. Who, or what, was a Plotmaster?

THAT'S RIGHT, LOUIE.
I KNEW YOU'D SEE THROUGH ME
SOONER OR LATER.

NOW WHAT SEEMS TO BE THE PROBLEM?

Louie quickly explained their problems with the ring, the ever-tightening cycle, and the Change. And, as he finished, he added that it was all his fault.

The booming fellow laughed.

OH, LOUIE!
A SIDEKICK CAN'T DO ANYTHING BAD!
LET ME SEE THAT RING, WON'T YOU?

The choir music rose around them, like someone had turned up a volume switch. Roger felt the ring gently twist its way out of his grip. It floated over to the Plotmaster.

After a moment, the music softened as the Plotmaster's voice boomed out again:

HERE.
LOOK.
THE RING'S BROKEN.
THERE'S A HAIRLINE CRACK.

Roger stared. Somehow, even though the Captain Crusader Decoder Ring floated over next to the Plotmaster, he could clearly see the crack across the face of the ring.

SEE?
IT'S NOT YOUR FAULT.
IT'S JUST THAT THESE THINGS
ARE MADE OUT OF CHEAP PLASTIC.
AND ONCE THEY BREAK?
WELL—
WAIT A SECOND.
I'LL GET YOU A NEW ONE.

Although it was difficult to follow his precise movements in the brilliant illumination, Roger thought the Plotmaster looked upward.

SID!
CAN WE GET A RING DOWN HERE?

He paused as if listening.

YEAH.
STANDARD MODEL.
BUT A NEW ONE, HUH?
NONE OF THIS RECONDITIONED STUFF.

The Plotmaster looked back in the direction of his visitors and shrugged his massive, white-clad shoulders.

YOU'VE GOT TO BE FIRM
WITH THESE ACCOUNTANT TYPES.

The choir got suddenly louder again, the kind of sonic shift you always got at the beginning of a television commercial.

Roger looked down at his hand.

He held a brand new Captain Crusader Decoder Ring.

The music faded.

The Plotmaster waved. He held something in his hand. Roger realized he was smoking a cigar. And oddly enough —or maybe it wasn't, considering the situation—in this strange illumination the cigar smoke looked blue.

WELL, IT'S BEEN A REAL PLEASURE
CHATTING WITH YOU BOYS.

"Wait!" Louie called. "There's so much we could ask you!"

The Plotmaster shook his light-haloed head.

BUT TIME IS MONEY.
I'VE GOT TO TAKE A MEETING.
LET'S DO LUNCH SOMETIME, HEY?

The well-lighted figure chuckled apologetically.

OF COURSE, YOU WON'T REMEMBER
ANY OF THIS.

He looked upward again.

SID!
I'VE GOT TO SEND SOME FRIENDS OF MINE
BACK INTO THE 'VERSE!
GET ME REWRITE!

He waved again, this time with finality.

CIAO, BOYS!

After that, all was blackness.

CHAPTER

⊿ 17 ⊿

It was much more peaceful when the smoke cleared. In fact, Roger might have called their new surroundings almost idyllic. They seemed to be on a brightly lit country road, the sun directly overhead, the sky a perfect blue.

Roger paused. Something was wrong. He couldn't remember exactly where they had come from. He remembered getting out of the war zone as quickly as they could. But after that—they had been on a pirate world, that was it! But why did he remember good robbers from the forest? Women with swords? Singing buccaneers?

And who, or what, was a Plotmaster?

He turned to ask Louie a question, but stopped when he saw the look of utter horror on the sidekick's face.

"Uh-oh," Louie said.

"What do you mean, uh-oh?" Roger asked. Was there something else around here that he didn't understand? "We're not being shot at or—or threatened with swords." Yes, he remembered the swords quite clearly now. He waved his hands at the perfect sky. "The sun's shining. Birds are singing. What's the matter around here? And, for

that matter, why did you use the ring in the middle of all
those pirates?"

"Pirates?" Louie blinked. "That's right, we were on a
pirate world, weren't we? Why don't I remember it better?
I guess your mind tries to blank out unpleasant things." He
looked down at the verdant lawn around his feet. "I have
this thing—about swords, you know. I couldn't worry
about the Change when my gizzard was about to be split."

Louie looked back at Roger. From the look on his face,
whatever they were facing now frightened him every bit as
much as swords. "But we don't have time to worry about
that—not anymore."

Doc nodded. "Sometimes a place can be too perfect."
He glanced distastefully at the guitar he still carried, as if
the instrument had turned into a rattlesnake.

From Doc's and Louie's reactions, Roger decided it was
too dangerous around here to take any time to ask about the
Plotmaster. He felt, somehow, that he should know all
about the Plotmaster already.

Music drifted from somewhere nearby.

"It's a wonderful day to be walking," a voice sang, "and
a wonderful day to be talking."

Doc nodded, "Just like I reckined."

"Oh, no," Louie moaned, "anywhere but here."

Roger decided he would feel better if his companions
would at least explain what was worrying them so much.

"What's the matter?" Roger insisted.

"Just try moving," Louie replied, "and you'll find out."

Roger lifted his right foot to take a step, and realized
what Louie meant. He felt as if he were walking through
molasses.

"Now," Louie said, "sing about what you're going to
do. And make it rhyme."

Roger did as he was told:

"Oh, I'm going to take a step!" he sang. "And I'll do it
with some pep!"

His foot seemed to move forward of its own accord.

"It's what I feared," Louie explained. "You've landed

us on the most unpredictable of all the worlds—the Musical Comedy!"

"*I* landed us!" Roger protested. He still held the ring, but Louie was the one who had called out the traveling orders from—from wherever they had come from.

But Louie was too upset to argue. "You've seen what it's like in musical comedy. Something's going one way, then suddenly the singing and dancing starts, and the plot turns around completely! Nothing stays the same in a place like this, and it'll suck you in before you know it. If you don't watch out every second, you'll be embroiled in a romantic subplot! Once that happens, you're stuck here— happily after after."

"Whether you want it or not?" Roger said, aghast. Until now, he had never considered how subversive musicals could be.

"Oh, you'll want it all right," Louie replied. "You'll sing, you'll dance, and forget all about Delores and the Change!"

"Oh, no, I won't!" Nothing could keep him from Delores. "I'll use the ring right now!" But Roger could barely lift his hand. He could hear the singing coming closer.

> "Here we come,
> Oh what fun,
> On a country walk!
> Howdy stranger,
> Let's be neighbors;
> Stay a while and talk!"

"Quick!" Louie whispered. "We've got to get out of here before they see us. If they invite us to a wedding or a county fair, we may never escape!"

"I'm trying," Roger replied between clenched teeth. "My arm won't work."

"Hey there!" the voices sang from around the bend. "Hey there! It's time for the fair! And don't be blue, there'll be a wedding, too!"

"What can I do?" Roger panicked.

"Oh, of course!" and Louie burst into song:

> "It's time to use the ring,
> It's time to use the ring.
> Excuse me while I sing;
> But it's time to use the ring!"

Roger got the idea. It was so obvious when you sang about it.

> "Don't want to lecture, don't want to scold,
> But both of you fellas better take hold,
> Don't crack a smile and don't shed a tear,
> Once I turn this ring, we're out of here!"

"All together, now!" he shouted, then all three sang as one:

> "See you in the funny papers,
> See you in the funny papers—"

What rhymed with funny papers?

"I don't mean the bunny capers—" Roger added.

They were surrounded by blue smoke.

"I've totally lost my bearings," Louie admitted. "But maybe, just maybe, this is the place."

Roger stared at their surroundings. They seemed to be in a jungle of some sort. Did that mean Delores was being held prisoner in a jungle?

He heard a high, trumpeting sound. The ground shook as something rumbled through the undergrowth, smashing trees, bushes, dwellings, other animals, and anything else that stood in its way.

"Oh, dear," Louie remarked. "That does sound an awful

lot like a fear-maddened elephant, doesn't it?"

Roger had to agree that it did.

"Pity," Louie added. "Then maybe this isn't the place."

Roger realized they had something more immediate to worry about. As trees collapsed along the jungle path before them, he saw that it was indeed a fear-maddened elephant—a fear-maddened elephant headed straight for them!

But then there was another sound, in the trees above them, a call older than recorded history:

"Bunga bonga blooie!"

Roger would recognize that blood curdling cry anywhere. In fact, he had—only the other day—heard that blood curdling cry throughout an entire triple feature.

"Oh, really?" Louie remarked as the fear-maddened elephant bore down upon them. He grinned as he glanced into the trees overhead. "This could get interesting."

CHAPTER

18

Roger's mouth fell open. It was Zabana, Prince of the Jungle! He landed in front of them, directly in the elephant's path!

"I know that fella," Doc answered.

"That fella," as Doc put it, was well over six feet tall, with broad, well-muscled, very tanned shoulders. In fact, all of that fella, save for his long blond hair and leopard-skin boxer shorts, was tanned a deep bronze, a color closer to metal than to flesh. The newcomer stood, still and silent as a statue, facing the onrushing elephant, heedless of the way the maddened animal's half-ton hooves shook the jungle floor.

Roger stared in disbelief. This whole Cineverse business had seemed a little too unreal, until now. There was no mistaking who stood before him. He had spent too many rainy Saturday afternoons glued to his TV, watching this very jungle giant. It had to be his boyhood hero. Roger could no longer contain himself.

"Zabana!" he called.

As if in answer, the blond giant beat upon his massive

chest, his voice ululating forth to confront the advancing elephant.

"Eegah! Eegah! Greech Karoo!"

The enraged pachyderm trumpeted again as it continued to stampede in their direction.

Zabana glanced over his shoulder at the assembled sidekicks. He smiled apologetically.

"Oops," he remarked. "Zabana make mistake. Is female elephant!" He turned back to the rapidly approaching beast, to beat upon his chest and scream once more:

"Egah! Egah! Tandalayo!"

The elephant stopped abruptly, scuffing its feet on the broken trees that littered its path. It trumpeted apologetically, then walked back the way it came.

"There!" the jungle giant shouted gleefully. "Zabana triumph again!" He beat upon his chest once more. "Bunga bonga blooie. Aieyeeaieyeyoo!"

That latest scream sent chills through Roger. He had, of course, heard that victory call a thousand times on those rainy Saturday afternoons, but never this close, this loud, this personal.

Big Louie whistled appreciatively. "Wow. You sure did that with style."

"Zabana have way with animals," the jungle prince replied. "Animals are my life."

"Zabana," Roger whispered, still quite overwhelmed. He had never imagined he would meet anyone like this in the Cineverse. Zabana was a real hero. He wondered if there was some way to recruit this jungle prince in their search for Delores.

"Hey, hombre!" Doc called. "Don't you remember me? We met in *Zabana Goes West*!"

But Zabana held up one massive palm for silence. He frowned up at the sky and sniffed the air, then quickly stepped over to a tree, pressing his ear against the bark.

He looked up at the sidekicks and nodded curtly. "Natives come!"

Natives? Roger knew what that meant. He had seen these confrontations often enough in the seventy-odd Zabana films he'd had the opportunity to watch. They were about to be visited by the proud, yet deadly, tribe that shared Zabana's jungle realm:

The Whatsahoosie!

Roger waited for the telltale beat of jungle drums, and the sound of fifty pairs of naked feet pounding their way up the forest path. He squinted out into the dense vegetation, eager despite himself for a first glimpse of the Whatsahoosie's ceremonial battle garb, replete with the multicolored feathers of tropical birds.

"Natives?" Louie muttered. "Big fellows, probably? With lots of sharp knives and spears? Who want to cut out our hearts because we unknowingly violated some obscure tribal ritual? Hey, I know how these places work." He looked imploringly at Roger. "You don't think it's time to use the ring, maybe?"

Roger shook his head. Now that he'd found an actual, honest-to-goodness hero, this was one place he didn't want to leave.

Louie looked unhappy with Roger's decision. Doc unslung his guitar and began to play short, menacing chords as he observed the surrounding jungle.

"Quiet!" Roger commanded in a hushed voice. "When the natives show up, we want to be ready for them."

He peered once again into the surrounding undergrowth. But he still couldn't see a thing, and all he could hear were the distant sounds of snapping twigs and muffled curses.

"Ow! Watch that branch, would you—"

"Bloody vegetation!"

"Ralph!"

"Bloody H—!"

"Would you calm down?"

"Sorry, George, old man. I just wish I could keep my briefcase from getting caught in these vines."

"We're almost there now—ah, just ahead!"

The vegetation parted before them, and three tall black men emerged, all of them wearing gray-pinstriped business suits.

"Well," the fellow in the lead announced genially, "here we are."

Another of the newcomers peered over his horn-rimmed glasses. "Say, isn't that the Zabana fellow?"

The jungle prince nodded at the business-suited three-some. "Me Zabana. You Whatsahoosie."

Roger couldn't help himself. "These are the Whatsa-hoosie?" he asked incredulously.

"Ah," the fellow in the lead smiled indulgently. "You are perhaps familiar with our old image. Back when we used to carry spears, beat drums, and wear all those parrot feathers?" He tsked softly as his right hand played with the knot on his pastel tie. "One has to keep up with the times, don't you know."

"Th-the times?" Roger sputtered. "But I remember you as fierce warriors, relentlessly pursuing your independence and tribal way of life!"

"Ah, but we are still fierce warriors," the leader replied smoothly. "It is just our battleground that has changed. But we should introduce ourselves. We are George"—he pointed to himself, then to his companion with the horn rims—"Ralph, and, over here, N'bonga."

The third Whatsahoosie sighed. "I am afraid some parents are still mired in the past. Rest assured, though—my friends call me Edgar."

Roger introduced his companions as well. Sidekicks and Whatsahoosie shook hands all around.

"You see," George continued once the introductions were completed, "things have changed in our jungle. After all, with all the money we had, what could we do but attend the most exclusive private schools in Whatsahoosie-land?"

"All the money?" Big Louie asked, suddenly interested in the conversation.

"Sure," George replied smoothly. "You know how Za-bana is. He's always going off and finding Lost Cities of Gold and Nazi treasure hordes. He just comes back here and dumps them, then goes off in the trees someplace to practice his animal calls."

"Animals are Zabana's friends," the jungle lord added agreeably.

"Whatever," George continued. "So, the Whatsahoosie decided to spend a little time on self-improvement. We are the proud results!"

Ralph snorted. "And still we have to come back to this bloody jungle!"

"Now, now," George chided. "You know we've come here with a purpose." He glanced about distractedly, finally pointing to his right. "Now, I see the shopping mall over there."

"Under the spreading giant palms?" N'bonga/Edgar observed from the rear. "Very nice. But what about that river?"

"Oh, no problem," George reassured him. "We simply pave it over."

"Capital idea," Ralph agreed. "It can be part of the parking lot."

"Wait a moment!" Roger interjected. "You're going to build a shopping mall? Here? In the middle of the jungle? What will happen to Zabana?"

"Not to worry, old shoe," Ralph replied. "We've planned that all out as well. Rest assured, Zabana will be an important part of our theme park."

"Hey!" Edgar chimed in. "Don't forget to tell them about our exclusive tree condos!"

"Most certainly," George agreed, checking a small notebook he had pulled from his briefcase. "And if you get in on the ground floor, we can give you substantial discounts!"

"A capital investment!" Ralph added.

"And have we mentioned our special time-sharing plan?" Edgar asked, reaching down to open his portfolio. "You may have already won—"

"Oh, no you don't!" another voice called from the trees.

"Friend to Zabana!" The jungle prince waved as the newcomer dropped from the trees into their midst. He was tall and well-muscled, his ebony skin glistening in the equatorial sun. Roger decided the newcomer's skin appeared even darker than it might otherwise because of the belt and armbands woven from multicolored parrot feathers. In other words, this fellow was dressed like a Whatsahoosie.

"Oh, man," Edgar muttered distractedly.

"Really," Ralph agreed. "Do you believe this fellow?"

"Quiet, young ones!" the newcomer thundered. "I have heard of your plans. So, you will rape the jungle for your shopping mall, and pave over the mighty Hoosomacallit River for a parking lot, then force the exalted Zabana to work in your theme park? This shall never be. So say I!" He glowered at his fellow tribesmen. "How do you answer that?"

The three other Whatsahoosie glanced at each other. George turned back to the newcomer.

"Oh, yeah?" he said. "And what are you gonna do about it?"

The newcomer fumed. "Do you not remember me as your great leader?"

"Our former great leader!" Edgar countered, glancing at the others in the clearing. "It's true. Back in our old tribal days, this fellow used to be the Grand Thingamabob."

The Thingamabob nodded pleasantly to Roger and the sidekicks. "You may call me Bob for short."

"That still doesn't change anything!" George countered.

Bob took a single step toward the three in business suits.

"Hey!" George exclaimed as he hastily backed away.

"We don't want any trouble here," Edgar added.

"I just got this suit cleaned." Ralph brushed his lapels protectively.

Bob sneered. "And you call yourselves Whatsahoosies!"

"Hey, man," Edgar objected. "We've just readjusted our priorities."

Something like a chuckle rumbled deep within the Thingamabob's throat. "Is that the name you give it now? Priorities? Well, I call you the lowest of the low—nothing more than money-grubbing animals!"

"Animals are Zabana's friends!" the jungle prince interjected.

Theme parks? Money-grubbers? This was like nothing Roger had ever seen in a Zabana film! Roger once again found himself nearly overwhelmed by these events. The change in the jungle was quite amazing.

But that was it—wasn't it?

"Excuse me, Bob," Roger interjected. "But did all this—the breakdown of the tribe, the new emphasis on money—"

"Dollars and cents," George agreed.

"The bottom line," Edgar added.

"Bloody right," Ralph chirruped.

Roger waved at the three financiers. "Did this happen because of the Change?"

"I think it began there," Bob answered. "Not that the Change was necessarily a bad thing. Let us face it. The old tribal way of life—what with days filled with hours of general spear-carrying, more hours of menacing effete white hunters, and even more hours shouting "Bad juju!" —could be somewhat limiting. So perhaps a change was due. However, I do not think it is the one the youngsters have chosen!"

"Oh, yeah?" George replied again.

"Have you done all that much better?" Ralph challenged. "Look what's happened to you and Zabana!"

"Is true," Zabana agreed sadly. "Family gone."

"Oh, no!" Roger blurted. "You mean Shirley—?"

Zabana nodded. "She now consultant in Congo."

His faithful female companion gone? Roger found this horribly traumatic. "And what about your son, Son?"

"Son go next jungle," Zabana admitted sadly. "Do own series—*Kanga, The Jungle Kid*." He shook his head sadly. "Life not easy for Prince of Jungle."

"Oh, dear," was all Roger could think to say. He decided it was better not to ask the whereabouts of Zabana's loyal orangutan, Oogie.

"Let's face it, fellows," Ralph concluded. "Zabana and the Thingamabob are both living in the past. Giving them jobs in our theme park would be doing them a favor!"

"Do not speak so soon!" The Grand Thingamabob thundered. "You act as if the jungle will let you pave it over without a battle! Do you not know that the jungle is a special place, and you must have special talents to conquer it?"

Doc strummed his guitar appreciatively. "Sounds like hero talk to me."

Roger had to agree. Perhaps they could recruit this Bob fellow as well, and they could have two heroes aiding in their quest to find Captain Crusader. Unless—

Roger looked speculatively at the blond Zabana, studying his manly physique, his square jaw, his slightly self-deprecating smile. Roger remembered that the last time they were around a hero, that hero turned out to be the actual Captain Crusader. What if the greatest hero in the Cineverse was once again in their midst—not as a masked marshal, but as a prince of the jungle?

"Oh, yeah?" George shot back at Bob. "If it's so tough around here, how do you survive?"

The blond giant nodded pleasantly. "Jungle is Zabana's friend!"

Everything seemed to be Zabana's friend. So much for that idea, Roger concluded. No, this jungle prince didn't seem to be quite up to the Captain Crusader level.

"And you must beware the jungle," Bob added solemnly, "for it will always surprise you!"

As if on cue, there was an explosion in their midst. A blue smoke explosion.

"Holy Toledo!" Big Louie exclaimed.

"Is it Doctor Dread?" Roger asked, trying to get a clear view through the smoke.

"Even worse," Louie answered. "It's my sister!"

CHAPTER

19

So Louie had been right after all. Dread had sent someone after the sidekicks to make sure they were—taken care of.

Roger heard Bertha's voice before he saw her.

"Well, boys," she drawled. "It's time to clean up some scum."

That's when the smoke cleared. Roger wished it hadn't. Bertha stood in the midst of a knot of men in double-breasted suits. All the men carried pistols, blackjacks, knives, brass knuckles, and various other instruments of destruction. Bertha held a machine gun. She smiled when she saw Roger.

"I'm going to clean some of this scum"—she paused significantly—"personally."

"*Now* is it time to use the ring?" Louie wailed.

"In a second." Roger still had to talk to Zabana and the Grand Thingamabob. If at all possible, he wanted the two heroes to leave with them.

Doc smiled as he put down his guitar. "First, we may have to do a little shootin'."

The double-breasted fellows had a good laugh at that

one. "You and what army?" one of them shouted.

"Zabana not need army!" the jungle prince announced. "Who challenges Zabana?"

This seemed to upset some of the henchmen.

"Zabana?"

"Doctor Dread didn't tell us about Zabana!"

"Pipe down," Bertha ordered. "Look on the bright side. It's not every day you get to clean up a jungle prince."

The double-breasted people laughed at that, and readied their weapons for battle.

The Grand Thingamabob shook a spear above his head. The shaft of wood was longer than a man was tall, brightly painted and ornamented with yellow and green feathers; its large metal head gleamed golden in the sun. It was quite an impressive spear. Roger wondered where Bob had gotten it.

"Step forward, and you shall feel the might of the Whatsahoosie!"

"The Whatsahoosie?"

"Now wait a minute!"

"First Zabana and now this?"

The henchmen's cheer seemed to have deserted them again.

Bertha waved her machine gun over the double-breasted throng. That's when Roger noticed the silver bracelets on her arm. They looked an awful lot like the bracelets clinking on Delores' arm the last time he'd seen her. Except, on Bertha, instead of hanging fashionably loose, they seemed to dig deeply into the fabric of her khaki fatigues, bunching up the cloth, and probably the skin beneath.

But if those bracelets were on Bertha now, what had happened to Delores? Roger realized, more than ever, how important it was to escape.

"Come on now, boys!" Bertha cheered. "Where's your villainous team spirit? There's a lot more than heroes to clean up around here. I mean, look at all those sidekicks!" She aimed her roscoe at the financiers. "Why don't we start by wiping out those three fellows in suits over there?"

"Perhaps," George admitted, "we should rethink our plans."

"It might not be a bad idea," Ralph concurred, "were we to find a quieter part of the jungle."

Edgar nodded as the three of them backed away. "I wonder how Kanga, the jungle kid, feels about tree condos?"

All three turned quickly and disappeared into the verdant undergrowth.

"See there?" Bertha crowed. "Nobody stands a chance against the forces of Doctor Dread!"

"Nobody?" Zabana shot back at the assembled evildoers. "Nobody not here! Here is Zabana! Here is Grand Thingamabob! Here are—" Zabana paused with a frown. He glanced at Roger and his fellows. "Zabana beg pardon. Not properly introduced."

Roger and the sidekicks introduced themselves.

"Much better!" the jungle prince declared. "All on first name basis! Now, where was Zabana? Oh, yes!" He pounded his chest a couple of times for effect. "Here is Zabana! Here is Grand Thingamabob! Here is Roger and Doc and Louie! Together, we defeat your evil plans, and all bad people who come to Zabana's jungle! Bunga bonga blooie!"

The next sound that came from Zabana's throat sounded—to Roger—like nothing so much as an alligator in heat.

"What was that?" one of the henchmen quavered.

"Whatever it was," Bertha said rather more forcefully, "you'd better not let him do it again."

There was a distant rumbling in the forest.

Zabana called out again, a noise akin to a hundred monkeys jamming a crosstown bus.

The rumbling grew louder.

"What did I say about letting him do this?" Bertha demanded.

"Okay, okay. I'm on my way."

The henchman stepped forward, luger at the ready.

The Grand Thingamabob stepped in front of him.

"It is not so simple as that," he rumbled. "To reach Zabana, you must pass me first."

"If that's the way you want it, buddy," the henchman sneered as he lifted his gun.

The long spear spun in Bob's hands, hitting the luger with a sharp crack. The gun went flying behind the nearby ferns.

"If you are going to carry a gun," Bob remarked dryly, "you should learn how to handle it."

The expression on the henchman's face was a mixture of fear and rage.

"W-w-why!" he sputtered. "I'm gonna—"

"Lefty!" Bertha barked. "Get back here! This is Moose's kind of job."

Zabana used this opportunity for another of his strange calls, this one rather like a group of crows trapped in a plummeting elevator. The rumbling noise answered back, still deep in the jungle.

Lefty scrambled back to Bertha's side as a much larger henchman lumbered forward, even more massive than the large cowpokes they had encountered earlier. It wasn't his height that was so exceptional, although he was certainly tall enough. It was the width of his shoulders that was so surprising, each a yard from the arms to the tree-stump neck. Of course, the fact that his arms hung down so low at his sides that his knuckles almost brushed the jungle floor, did nothing to diminish the feeling that they were facing a human engine of destruction.

"Moose," Bertha instructed. "We have some vermin here for you to stomp—" She paused, then added, "to rip—" She smiled as she amended, "—to pummel."

The incredibly large person stopped. His mouth opened as he looked at Roger and his fellows. From deep in his throat came a single, monosyllabic grunt. Only then did the massive thug once again lumber forward. The noise seemed to have taken all his concentration.

Zabana cut loose with the most elaborate call of all, something that started like fifty parrots asking for a wide variety of crackers, but finished more like a troupe of laughing hyenas swallowing numerous bullfrogs.

The rumbling sound was much closer. As it approached, it sounded much more like a hooting, howling, trumpeting, roaring, rumbling. Roger thought he felt the jungle floor shake beneath his feet.

Bertha ignored it. "Moose," she instructed, "when you stomp, rip, and pummel all of these scum, spare that worthless toadie over in the corner." She smiled at Roger. "That one is mine."

"Uuhhh," Moose replied.

Then the Grand Thingamabob stepped in his path.

"It is not so simple as that. To reach the others, you must pass—"

Moose reached forward with lightning speed and ripped the spear from Bob's hands. The large man flexed his knuckles. The spear broke in half.

"Uuhhh," Moose remarked.

"Remember, Moose," Bertha called as she pointed to Roger. "This scum is mine." She paused, letting her tongue roll over her teeth. "Maybe I'll go slow and let him last a day or two."

"Uuhhh," Moose agreed.

The Grand Thingamabob did not move from the large man's path. "If I must die," he announced, "I will die as a Whatsahoosie!"

"No one die here!" Zabana objected. "No one but bad people. Help is on way!"

Roger realized that the rumbling had redoubled. And the hooting, hollering, braying, cawing, and trumpeting was getting so loud it was hard to hear Zabana at all.

"Animals are Zabana's friends!" the jungle prince announced.

"Uuhhh," Moose remarked uncertainly.

For the animals were upon them. And what a group of animals they were. In movie after movie, Roger had seen the jungle prince call one animal or another to get him and his friends out of one scrape or another. In *Zabana's Jungle Fountain* he had called upon the lions and other great cats, and sure enough, here were lions and leopards and jaguars again leaping into the clearing. In *Zabana Versus the Nazi Death Ray*, the prince had summoned a stampede of jungle wart hogs to wipe out the German patrol, and here, once again, Roger could hear the characteristic snorting over the pounding sound of a hundred wart hog hooves. In *Zabana and His Son* it had been water buffaloes; in *Zabana's Water Adventure*, man-eating crocodiles; in *Zabana Versus the Communist Menace* (one of his later, lesser films), crazed rhinoceroses. And then there were all those films where he brought in the elephants in the final reel. But Roger had never seen all the animals on the rampage all at once. At least, he hadn't until now.

Apparently, for this particular occasion, Zabana had called out everything.

"Into trees, friends!" Zabana instructed.

Roger did as he was told, quickly climbing into the lower branches of a gnarly oak as the first of the animals thundered by below him. He saw both Louie and Doc were climbing trees nearby.

"Get back here, Moose!" Bertha hollered. But Moose had already disappeared from sight, overwhelmed by the wild herd. Perhaps he was trampled, or perhaps he merely joined the stampede; it was impossible for Roger to see. Whatever had happened, he was gone.

Roger saw that the herd, which, until then, had consisted mostly of the big cats, antelopes, water buffaloes, wart hogs, and the occasional giraffe, was tending toward larger and larger animals as it passed on by—here a hippo, there a rhino, and taking up the rear—the elephants. Perhaps, Roger considered, there was a reason both Zabana and Bob had retreated to the upper branches. Roger climbed again, swiftly but carefully, cautious not to be knocked from his safe perch by the earthquake stampeding below.

That same stampede had almost reached Dread's rapidly retreating henchpeople.

"We're not done with you yet!" Bertha glared at Roger meaningfully. "I'm especially not done with you! Gather around me, lackies!"

The henchmen clustered around Bertha as she used her ring. An instant later, they were gone.

"Animals Zabana's friends." The jungle prince smiled. "Animals also good solution to many everyday problems. Save messy cleanup afterward, too."

Roger looked down at the forest floor as the last of the elephants passed. All the underbrush, and everything else that had been down there, was gone, pressed into a green and brown pulp. Zabana was right. There *was* nothing left down there to clean up.

"Is it safe to climb back down?" Roger asked.

"Wait a second," the jungle prince cautioned. He called out again, this noise eerily like an air raid siren crossed with the songs of jungle birds.

He stopped and nodded at Roger. "Safe now. Zabana give all clear."

Roger shimmied down the tree, and joined the others on the flattened forest floor.

"I am glad we were able to save our new-found friends," The Grand Thingamabob said with a smile. "There are few enough heroes left. We cannot squander them."

"Shucks," Doc offered. "We're not heroes. We're only sidekicks, looking to get by."

Roger saw his chance to make his pitch.

"Exactly," he hurriedly added, rapidly explaining that they had sworn to defeat Doctor Dread and at the same time rescue a lady in distress. He looked at both heroes as he concluded: "We could use your help."

The Grand Thingamabob shook his head with a smile. "So you will never be heroes—that's what you think? And are you sure that heroes have to be born that way, that they cannot rise to the circumstance?" He paused, considering his own question. "Well, perhaps it was that way, before the Change."

"Change?" Zabana pondered the issues as well. "Yes, jungle prince will come. You saw what happen with local people." The blond giant sighed. "Place not same. Zabana think he could use change of jungle."

"Good!" Roger said enthusiastically. He turned to the Grand Bob. "And you?"

Bob shook his head sadly. "Alas, I cannot. I am needed elsewhere. But we will meet again." He waved to all of them a final time. "And remember—never leave your rhino meat outside to dry."

Roger felt a shiver flow down his spine as he glanced at the others. Never leave your rhino meat? Wasn't that the sort of thing you'd hear in a Whatsahoosie social studies class? Or the kind of message you might have decoded if you were staying in the jungle and using a plastic ring that was also the key to the Cineverse?

Roger decided he had to ask. But the Grand Thingama-bob was gone. Somehow, without a sound, he had faded back into the jungle.

"Was that—?" he began anyway.

Doc nodded before Roger could finish. "Who else could it be?"

Big Louie agreed. "Yeah, that looked like a hero's hero."

So that was Captain Crusader? Roger smashed a fist into his open palm. So close—and now he was gone! True, he hadn't looked much like the Masked Marshal, but shouldn't Roger have been able to recognize him by his noble actions? Why hadn't Roger at least added that they were also looking for him?

"He always shows up where you least expect him," Louie added, trying to be cheerful.

"But we've lost him," Roger replied, not caring if the others heard the hint of despair in his voice. "What can we do now?"

"No problem," Louie replied, blowing on his knuckles. "Now that I know we've landed in Zabana's jungle, I know where to go next. If I may tell you how to set the ring?"

Roger nodded, realizing they had to go on—for De-lores, if nothing else. This time, he listened carefully to Louie's instructions before he made a move.

CHAPTER

⚜ 20 ⚜

At first, Roger thought something had gone wrong. When the blue smoke cleared, the jungle was still there. But the blue smoke had vanished in an instant, blown away by a sea breeze. And the jungle floor was no longer trampled underfoot, but seemed even more lush and green than it had before.

Roger realized they were in a brand new jungle. And— for some reason—his confusion brought forth images of men with swords, and—for that matter—women with swords, and pirates, and buccaneers who didn't seem all that different from the pirates, except that the buccaneers did a lot of singing.

Singing? Where did that come from?

And who, or what, was the Plotmaster?

"We're here," Louie commented tersely.

"Oh," Roger replied, explaining his confusion.

Zabana nodded his agreement. "You see one jungle, you see them all."

"Yeah," Louie countered, "but this place is different.

Can't you smell the sea? Can't you hear the noise of distant drums?"

Now that the diminutive sidekick mentioned it, Roger could hear a faint rhythm beneath the swish of windblown palm fronds.

"It come from beach," Zabana said wisely.

"Drums?" Doc asked uncertainly. "Those aren't like Indian war drums, are they?"

"On a peaceful South Sea island like this?" Big Louie scoffed. "You've got to be kidding."

"Never speculate on natives," Zabana commented, "until you properly introduced."

Roger realized that he didn't have time to worry about pirates or Plotmasters. Now that they were here, he had only one goal. He had to rescue Delores!

"Well, I think the natives will have to wait," Roger interrupted. "Louie, you got us here. Now get us to Doctor Dread."

"Oh, that." Louie smiled sheepishly. "Well, um, there is a little—uh—problem."

"Wait a moment," Roger replied. "Are you telling me you don't know Dread's whereabouts?"

"Well, sure I know," Louie said defensively. "He's on this island. I just don't know—uh—quite where on this island."

Roger frowned, pausing long enough to tuck the Captain Crusader Decoder Ring safely in his jacket pocket. "Hold on here. How do you know he's on this island in the first place?"

Louie shrugged. "Hey, my sister used to talk to me, you know?"

But Roger wasn't going to let Louie off that easily. "So if she told you, why didn't she give you the exact location?"

"Exact location?" Louie stared with sudden interest at the undergrowth surrounding his Western boots. "I'm afraid my sister and I weren't *that* close."

Roger sighed and looked heavenward. "Where does that leave us?"

"Well, I figure he's got to be someplace on this island," Louie insisted. "I mean, how big can a South Sea island be, anyway?"

"Pardon me, fellas," Doc drawled, "but aren't those drums getting closer?"

Roger paused. Doc was right. The rhythmic pounding was much louder than before. What could it mean? What had it meant in all those old movies Roger had seen? A great many different things, as he recalled. And most of those things, as he remembered, were none too healthy for the heroes. Roger once again felt a bit of panic trying to escape.

"What do they want?" he asked, his voice much lower than before.

"Maybe natives hear us," Zabana said reasonably.

Roger bit his lip. It was true. Heaven knew, Roger and Louie had made no attempt to be discreet in their argument.

The drums were booming through the jungle now.

"But what do they really want?" he asked again.

"Never speculate on natives—" Zabana began.

Roger cut him off with a curt nod. Of course the jungle prince was right. But until they knew the natives' motives, the wise thing to do would be to keep out of their way.

"I suggest that we start looking for Dread's hideout," Roger suggested, "say—in any direction but where the drums are coming from?"

That sounded like a good idea to everybody else. They moved, as quickly and quietly as the jungle would allow, away from the persistent drumbeats. Roger waved at Zabana to lead the way. The jungle prince bounded quickly to the front of the line.

They had traveled only another fifty feet or so when Zabana raised a hand for the party to halt. The jungle prince looked back at the others.

"People ahead," he whispered.

"Is it the native drummers?" Roger whispered back.

Zabana shook his head. "They still beating somewhere

behind us. These not natives. These people from some-place else!"

Someplace else? Roger's breath caught below his Adam's apple. Could they have found Dread's hideout already? Was his search finally at an end?

He quickly strode past Zabana. Delores could be up there! He hoped she hadn't been treated too badly. If Dread had done anything to her, Roger swore the evil mastermind would pay!

The palm trees seemed to be thinning out ahead. There was a clearing in the midst of the jungle, and in the middle of that clearing was a single, great tree. And tied to that tree was a woman wearing a black vinyl jump suit, but no bracelets. A woman with long blond hair. A woman Roger would know anywhere.

Delores!

Roger ran forward, toward the last copse of palms that ringed the clearing. Dried bamboo shoots cracked beneath his jogging shoes. So much for the silent approach. Still, there didn't seem to be anyone else around. Maybe he could quickly untie Delores and the two of them could just as quickly escape before her captors returned.

That's when Delores saw him. But she didn't look happy to see him. In fact, she appeared to be rather annoyed.

"Roger!" she called. "What are you doing here?"

He grinned. "I've come to rescue you!"

She seemed horrified by the thought. "Rescue? Who wants to be rescued?"

"Don't you?" he replied, a bit taken aback. "You are tied to a tree!"

Delores attempted to shrug her shoulders within her roped confines. "Who says I don't want to be tied to a tree?" She glanced about distractedly. "Look, Roger, don't you have something better to do?"

"Better? But, Delores, after all we've meant to each other? I thought—"

"That was your problem," she interrupted. "Thinking."

She suddenly smiled. Roger's heart lifted. Had she been teasing him all along?

"Oh, you didn't tell me you'd brought company along," she said coquettishly. "Handsome company!"

It was only then that Roger realized he had a jungle prince at his side.

"Sorry to interrupt," Zabana murmured. "But what we do about drummers?"

Now that Zabana mentioned it, Roger realized the drumming was getting very loud indeed.

"What should we do?" he asked, upset and confused as much by Delores' reactions as by any imminent danger.

The jungle prince frowned in thought for an instant.

"Zabana distract!" He waved to Roger, then disappeared into the jungle.

"What?" Delores demanded, frowning again now that the jungle prince was gone. "Not only are you trying to untie me against my wishes, you're going to let your hand-some friend go without even introducing me?"

Roger had had enough of this nonsense. "No, Delores. I'm coming for you!"

Delores shrieked. "If you take another step closer to me, Roger, it will be your life!"

She glanced at the trees to her left. "Um—I mean, it'll be the end of our life together!"

What was going on here? Every time Delores opened her mouth, Roger ended up more upset than before. This went far beyond mere playfulness. Had Dread done some-thing to Delores' mind?

Perhaps, he considered, he should use some reverse psychology. If she thought she was going to lose him, surely Delores would change her mind.

Roger sighed. "Well, then, all I can do is leave."

He took a slow and exaggerated step away.

"If you want it that way," she agreed all too readily. "I might as well be plain. I never want to see you again, Roger. I'm going to stay with Doctor Dread the rest of my life!"

What did she mean? He took a step back toward her. This didn't make any sense at all.

"Do you know what you're saying?" he demanded.

"I certainly do," Delores agreed. "And you know what I'd do if I were you? I'd be so mad, I'd take that ring and get out of here—back where you belong!" Her eyes wandered once again toward the trees to her left. Her gaze snapped back to Roger. Did she look the slightest bit feverish?

"Just think how much simpler your life was," she continued, forcing a smile, "before you met me. Why don't you be a good guy and zap yourself back to Earth—right away!"

Back before he met her? Back when he was dating Sandra? Or even worse, Phyllis? No matter how many times she tried to get rid of him, he still couldn't believe it. "Delores, do you know what you're saying?"

But all she could do was groan. "Oh, Roger, you can be so thickheaded! Get out of here, now!"

Roger turned away. What could he do but leave? He turned away, despondent. He thought he heard someone sobbing softly behind him. Roger knew it must be his imagination—one last instance of wishful thinking from a man who'd wasted his life at the movies. It couldn't be Delores. Not after the way she'd treated him.

Roger heard two noises in the distance. One, of course, was the drums. The other was a call not unlike a tiger attempting the falsetto part of a doo-wop ballad. Zabana must be out there somewhere, distracting.

Louie and Doc waited for him a few paces back within the jungle.

"Tough break, pardner," Doc commiserated.

"Why would she do this to me?" Roger asked, not really expecting an answer.

"Maybe she likes it that way," Louie suggested gently.

"What?" Roger asked incredulously. "Being tied up?"

"Well, you know," Louie continued apologetically, "maybe you hadn't gotten to that part of the relationship yet. Sometimes it takes a while to get to the—kinky stuff."

"Really?" Roger replied miserably. Actually, his relationship with Delores had been hot and heavy for some months. At least, that's how he remembered it. As he recalled, they had explored a lot of the kinky stuff already. But maybe Delores had had other ideas. He sighed. What did it matter now, anyway?

"What do we do now?" he asked his fellows listlessly.

"I think it's time for us to get lost," Doc suggested, "in a hurry!"

What did he mean?

Roger looked up.

"Huh?" he managed.

Louie shrugged. "The cowpoke's long gone."

Doc was nowhere to be seen. He had taken his own advice and disappeared into the undergrowth.

Wasn't that drum sound awfully close?

"What's going on here?" Roger ventured, his misery giving way to fear.

"Ah!" a deep voice boomed. "There you are!"

"Uh-oh," Louie whispered. "I don't think we should be. Here, that is."

Both Roger and Louie turned to face the newcomer.

He was tall and well-muscled, the shell necklace he wore brilliant white against his warm brown skin. Besides his jewelry, he wore nothing but a short skirt of dried grasses. Still, his smile was broad and genuine. He certainly seemed friendly.

And he led a group of islanders, fifty strong.

Before Roger could make any sort of decision about all this, the islanders surrounded them. Roger noticed that a large number of their greeting party were female, and very attractive besides. The women all wore sarongs with multicolored floral patterns and necklaces of bright woven flowers, while their faces were framed by glistening dark hair that hung to their waists. They smiled, too. In fact, everybody but Roger and Louie seemed to be smiling.

One of the women stepped forward, lifting her flowered necklace over her head. She placed it gently over Roger's head and onto his shoulders, then kissed his cheek.

"Welcome to our island paradise!"

Actually, Roger thought, this wasn't all that bad. A second woman approached, flowered necklace in hand. Roger waited patiently as she, too, placed the wreath of flowers on his shoulders and kissed him, this time on the other cheek. Yes, he could definitely get used to this. Let Delores reject him! Maybe he'd find his very own island beauty instead.

"We thought we would never find you!" the young lovely breathed.

No, no, this didn't seem bad at all. Maybe, Roger considered, being on the run on world after world in the Cineverse had made him too cautious, even paranoid.

He remembered his confusion over the swashbucklers, and that Plotmaster stuff. Heck, he could even be having delusions! And little wonder, too, the way he'd been jumping from world to world. Perhaps, now that Delores was gone—Roger tried to ignore the pain in his heart—what he really needed was a nice, long rest, in someplace sunny, someplace warm, someplace with dozens of beautiful distractions.

When he thought about it that way, it made a whole lot of sense. It would be a shame if his caution kept him from truly enjoying an island paradise.

Still, he remembered Zabana's warnings about the local populace. He wasn't sure exactly why these islanders were being that friendly. What—for example—if these people were in league with Doctor Dread, and had mistaken Roger and Louie for henchmen? No, before he relaxed completely, he had to ask a couple of questions.

"Are you sure it was us you were looking for?" he ventured cautiously. "Aren't there some other people on this island?"

"Other people?" one of the lovely women asked with a smile. "What need have we for other people?"

But one of the men added: "Oh, yeah. There is that guy in the tree making all those weird noises. Lucky we heard you yelling at that woman up here or we might have been distracted."

Well, it all seemed innocent enough. So why wasn't Roger enjoying himself more? Could he still, even now, have some leftover guilt about Delores? He laughed bitterly. Why should he feel anything for that woman, after she had just told him she was leaving him for Doctor Dread? Roger decided he had to readjust his priorities. And what better priority could there be than an attractive island beauty?

"So now it is time to go?" asked another of the saronged young women. "Yes?"

"Yes," Roger replied, deciding it truly was time to fully enjoy whatever this island had to offer. "Where?"

"We will take you down to the bright blue ocean," the beauty replied, "and introduce you to the rest of our friendly and fun-loving people."

"Oh," Roger replied, genuinely pleased. "That sounds nice."

Big Louie, however, apparently wasn't as convinced. "Then what happens?" he asked, a slight quaver to his voice.

Another of the women answered: "Then we will honor you with a great feast, which shall go on from sunset to sunrise."

"Oh," Louie admitted. "I guess Roger's right. That doesn't sound bad."

"Then," another of the lovelies added happily, "of course, we will sacrifice you to the Volcano God."

"Wakka Loa," one of the men added cheerfully. Drums beat in the distance.

BOOM *Boom* Boom boom.

The smiling well-muscled men grabbed both of Roger's arms in viselike grips.

"It is a great honor," they added.

Roger noticed that Louie was similarly pinioned.

"It happens very quickly," a beautiful woman said with a smile.

"And they use a very sharp knife," another added helpfully.

"Absolutely nothing to worry about," the man who

spoke first concluded. "Is everybody ready?"

And with that, their entire escort burst into song.

Roger was too preoccupied to listen to the words. Sacrifice? Volcano God? Perhaps this wasn't such a cheerful place after all. Roger tried to struggle, but it was useless. The islanders' grip was too tight, and they were moving too fast.

Louie and Roger were hustled, by the happy, singing islanders, all the way back to the beach.

CHAPTER

⟁ 21 ⟁

"Oh, it's awful, awful nice,
 Wakka Heenie, Wakka Ho,
 In our island paradise!
 Wakka Heenie, Wakka Ho.
 We're so glad that you've been found,
 Wakka Heenie, Wakka Ho,
 Cause we'd like to show you round,
 Wakka Heenie, *Unhhh!*"

Actually, Roger thought, this wasn't that bad. Here he was, being carried down to a tropical beach by two pairs of strong hands, surrounded by beautiful, smiling women, his mind pleasantly lulled by the exotic rhythms of the song they sang—sort of a cha-cha, mambo type of thing. Now, if he could just forget about being sacrificed to the Volcano God—

Roger blinked. He was going to be sacrificed to the Volcano God! What had he been thinking about? How could he have been lulled by anything when he was soon to be cut up in honor of some pagan deity? This was serious! Somehow, he had to get out of here.

The islanders began to sing again:

> "Not a thing you have to do,
>   Wakka Heenie, Wakka Ho.
> Lovely maidens sing for you,
>   Wakka Heenie, Wakka Ho.
> Everything's within our reach,
>   Wakka Heenie, Wakka Ho.
> 'Cause we're gonna hit the beach,
>   Wakka Heenie, *Uunnhhh!*"

Roger sighed. The music was awfully pleasant, no matter what was going to happen later—its lilting beat was as infectious as anything he had ever heard. His feet began to move, almost of their own volition, as if they wished to dance along. The women smiled at him. They had such nice smiles. Roger sighed again. He didn't know when he had ever been this happy.

The jungle ended, and the natives ran Roger out onto a beach of white sand that stretched from the lush forest out to the turquoise sea. But they had stopped singing.

And he was going to be sacrificed to a volcano god! He should be in a perpetual state of panic, not dancing along with the music. What was wrong with him?

"The same thing that's wrong with me," Louie answered from where he had been deposited by Roger's side. Oddly enough, Roger couldn't remember asking the question—at least, not out loud.

"What do you mean?" Roger asked back, rubbing his arms where they had so recently been gripped. But before Louie could answer, both were surrounded by a bevy of laughing young island beauties, who drew the two sidekicks farther down the beach, until Roger and Louie faced an islander of advanced years—an elder with skin like wrinkled leather, and hair as white as the snow these people would never see.

The elder smiled graciously. "Glad you could make it."

All the beauties began to talk at once:

"We are so happy to see you!" the beauties said.

"Enjoy our pristine beaches—" the elder added.

"Welcome to our island paradise!" the lovelies cheered.

"Bathe in our azure ocean—" the elder encouraged.

"We hope to make your stay as pleasant as possible," the maidens suggested.

"Visit with our cheerful local population—" the elder encouraged.

"There will be a feast in your honor," the women enthused.

"Sample the excellent local cuisine—" the elder mentioned.

"And then of course, the ultimate honor!" the maidens cooed.

"And," the elder agreed, "for a final thrill, there's a visit to the local volcano—"

The other islanders joined in as he spoke the next two words.

"Wakka Loa!"

BOOM *Boom* Boom boom, the drums said.

Roger had heard that noise before. He couldn't help himself. Sacrifice or no sacrifice, he had to ask:

"Do the drums always do that?"

"You try it," the elder suggested with a smile.

"Try what?" Roger asked.

"You know," a nearby beauty urged.

"Wakka Loa?" Roger guessed.

BOOM *Boom* Boom boom, the drums replied. The islanders cheered.

"Now you are truly one of us!" the elder exclaimed.

"The drums always do that," the beauty explained. "It is one of the many unique features of our island paradise."

"But you must have had a long and arduous journey to our pleasant vacation home under the sun." The elder pointed to a hut farther down the beach. "You should rest and refresh yourselves with some of our many and varied native delicacies."

Roger glanced at Big Louie.

"Yeah, why not?" the small fellow said.

Roger agreed. If he and Louie had to escape later, they might as well do it with full stomachs.

"Very good," the elder remarked as he led the way. "Later, we will amuse and fascinate you with a demonstration of some of our quaint island customs. And who could forget an evening of sensuous native dancing?"

Roger and Louie followed the elder into the hut, which was constructed from dried palm fronds covering a bamboo skeleton. The hut was surprisingly roomy inside. Four torches hung at regular intervals from the circular wall, illuminating a great table covered by an enormous variety of foodstuffs.

"The happy visitors are confronted by an amazing array of island treats," the elder commented. "What shall they sample first? The whole roast pig looks particularly scrumptious. Oh, but how about all those succulent fruits, picked fresh from the trees?"

Roger opted for a sliced pineapple and a cup of coconut milk, while Louie attacked the pig with a very large, very sharp knife.

"Wnnt smmme?" Louie asked from his full mouth, waving the blade in Roger's direction. Roger declined the offer. Under the present circumstances, he didn't want to have anything at all to do with very large, very sharp knives.

The elder waited patiently until they were done.

He spoke after both of them had put down their plates: "Their bellies full of island treats, the visitors wonder what's next on the agenda of their trip to this tiny paradise? They don't have long to wonder, though, because when they emerge from the hut, the evening's entertainment is in full swing!"

Roger frowned. Evening's entertainment? When they had walked into the hut, it had been the middle of the afternoon. It couldn't be that late, could it? He figured he needed all the time he could get to think of a way to escape this mess.

But when he stuck his head out of the hut, the sun had

indeed disappeared, replaced by the moon, the stars, and a score of saronged women doing the hula.

Roger frowned. Where had all the time gone? It seemed like one minute it was broad daylight, the next full night. It was just like a jump-cut in a movie.

In a movie? Roger's dinner growled ominously in his stomach as he realized another truth about the Cineverse. Some, if not all, of these worlds must work on movie time. And, on movie time, a whole life could pass in an hour and a half!

There was so much in the Cineverse he still didn't understand. Roger pushed recurring thoughts of the Plotmaster out of his mind. His current plight was much more serious than he had previously thought. He had to get away as soon as possible. There was no time for planning. He and Louie might have no time at all! One more jump-cut, and it would be sacrifice time!

"Are you thinking what I'm thinking?" Louie whispered in Roger's ear.

"You mean," Roger whispered back, "now that we're fed, it might be time to travel? Before we end up as a meal for a volcano?"

The elder smiled over at them. "Ah, but our visitors appear the slightest bit restless. I think it's time for a little more of that seductive native music."

The islanders obliged:

> "If you see the island dance,
>   Wakka Heenie, Wakka Ho.
>   You know the way we find romance,
>   Wakka Heenie, Wakka Ho.
>   Ah, perhaps—but we digress,
>   Wakka Heenie, Wakka Ho.
>   For you should sit there and digest!
>   Wakka Heenie, *Uunnnhhh*!"

Roger and Louie both sat down with satisfied sighs. What was the big hurry about, anyway? Now that he thought of it, Roger had always wanted to spend a quiet evening watching twenty hula dancers strut their stuff. So what if he was going to be sacrificed tomorrow? He'd worry about that when it happened. Tonight, he would be entertained!

The hula dancers stopped at last, and were replaced by four men who did a complicated juggling dance involving a large number of burning torches and long, sharp knives. Roger felt the slightest stirring of something at the very back of his mind. Wasn't there something about long, sharp knives that he should be thinking about? Oh, well. Maybe he'd figure it out when he finished watching these guys throw all that dangerous stuff around.

"Don't you fellas worry at all," a voice drawled close to his ear. "I'll have you out of here in less time than it takes to throw a steer."

Roger started out of his funk. It was Doc, here to rescue them. Rescue them? That's right, they were going to be sacrificed to the Volcano God! What could he have been thinking of?

"That's just it," Louie replied. "Neither of us were. Thinking, that is. These people here have got us under some sort of spell."

"Spell?" Doc whispered. "You fellas look plumb fine to me."

"Well, it's gone, now that you're here," Roger explained, realizing Louie was right. "But it is a trance of some sort, something we fall into and don't realize we're in—until we snap out of it again!"

Doc nodded knowingly. "Sort of like a three-day drunk."

"So, have you and Zabana come to rescue us?" Louie asked.

"Nope," Doc answered. "It's just me. Zabana's gone off somewhere. I reckon it was something about getting help with the drums or something. Sometimes I have trouble understanding that jungle fellow. Sure wish he used more verbs. Anyway, I figured I should step back in, with you guys about to be sacrificed and all, and try to lend you a hand. Thought my six-gun might come in handy." Roger heard the telltale click-click-click of a revolving cylinder.

"Thanks," Roger whispered appreciatively. "If you hadn't come, we would have been breakfast for Wakka Loa."

BOOM *Boom* Boom boom, the drums replied.

"What's that?" the elder asked as he turned away from the dancers. "Why, we have a new visitor to our tranquil island of delight. See how he, too, is overcome by the jubilant native welcome!"

Doc was grabbed by a dozen hands. His struggles were useless.

"But none of our island greetings would be complete," the elder added, "unless they were delivered in song!"

Song? Roger thought. Suddenly it became crystal clear —song seemed as much a force here as it was in the dread Musical Comedy!

"That's it!" he shouted. "That's where the trance is coming from. The music is doing it; that damn seductive music!"

But the islanders had already burst into song:

> "Oh, we welcome you anew,
> Wakka Heenie, Wakka Ho.
> To our island rendezvous,
> Wakka Heenie, Wakka Ho."

Roger could feel himself slipping away. But what was so bad about that?

"It'sh not sheductive!" Doc wailed. "It'sh intoxshicating!" The gun fell from his senseless fingers. A strange smile on his face, the Westerner pulled the guitar from his back and began to strum along.

> "Welcome to our isle romance,
> Wakka Heenie, Wakka Ho.
> Now sit back and watch us dance,
> Wakka Heenie, *Unnhh!*"

Yes, Roger thought, that wasn't such a bad idea, watching twenty smiling women in bright-colored sarongs. He was glad they were back—he liked their dance much better than the thing with the knives. It was nice that Doc could come along, too, and enjoy the entertainment.

Roger blinked. There was a line of pink in the eastern sky. Dawn? Had the entire night gone by already? Why did he find it so upsetting? Maybe he wanted the wonderful dancing and singing to go on forever!

"And what a wonderful place is this island paradise," the elder intoned, "a place where both natives and villagers would live every night as if it were their last!"

There was something about the old man's commentary that sent a cold chill through Roger. He wished the music would start again so he could forget whatever it was that was bothering him. Four men—the same ones who had previously danced with knives and torches—led another outsider into their midst, this one a woman.

"We are joined by another pilgrim on her jubilant march to destiny. The more the merrier, we always say!"

Roger blinked. He knew this so-called pilgrim. She was the same one who—the day before—had turned him down for Doctor Dread! And, even more upsetting, any time now, he was going to be sacrificed to a volcano god!

Delores caught his eye as she was hustled into their midst. She shrugged and smiled.

"And speaking of marches," the elder continued, "what a beautiful day it is for a march of our own. For our visitors will soon realize that no trip to our island is complete without a visit to our volcano god!"

"Wakka Loa!" the islanders cheered together.

BOOM *Boom* Boom boom, the drums added as the sun rose to light the way to Roger's death.

CHAPTER

⟁ 22 ⟁

The islanders urged Roger and his fellows to their feet, turning them away from the beach, toward a zigzag path that led up a steep incline. Roger didn't struggle. He knew, if he showed the least resistance, the elder would just get the rest of them to sing again. And Roger feared that song could make him do anything.

"But what's Delores doing here?" he whispered to Louie and Doc.

"I reckon maybe these were the folks that had her tied up to that tree," Doc ventured.

Could that be? Roger frowned in thought. If she was in that type of danger, why hadn't she asked for help? But no, she had laughed at his offer of assistance, and told him to forget her. Even worse, she had told him she had found another!

Roger had had trouble like this before. His relationship with Sheila was almost a carbon copy, and his abortive affair with Greta held some similarities as well, although Roger was pretty sure the current situation wouldn't involve a sheep named Otto. Whatever—he'd simply been

hurt too many times by too many women. He had thought
Delores was different, but now—

Roger sighed. When his life had sunk this low, maybe
they'd be doing him a favor by sacrificing him to the Volcano God.

"Reckon she couldn't do nothing else," Doc continued,
"what with those fellas hiding off in the bushes, waiting for
you to come out and rescue her."

"Fellows?" Roger repeated. "Hiding in the bushes?"

"Yep." Doc nodded. "Thought you might have seen
'em. 'Course, you don't have my experiences as an Indian
tracker. Then again, those fellas might not have had to take
a step if you had walked into one of those lion pits."

"Lion pits?" Roger replied.

"Yep." Doc spit ruminatively. "That's what Zabana
called them when he spotted them from the trees. Were at
least four of them pits out there, each seven feet deep, and
filled with six-foot bamboo spikes. Don't know why they
dug them, though. Haven't seen a lion since we showed up
on this island."

"Fellows with weapons?" Roger asked no one in particular. "Pits with spikes?" Perhaps Delores hadn't rejected
him after all. Could she have been trying to warn him
away? He looked ahead at the woman of his dreams, long
blond hair streaming past her bravely squared shoulders.
Oh, how could he have doubted her? How had he shut her
out of his life, even for a moment? How he longed to look
into her eyes and hear the sound of his name formed on her
sweet lips. He shrugged off the hands of his guards and
trotted forward, rapidly climbing the broad path. Nothing
would keep him from talking with her!

The elder cleared his throat as Roger passed:

"Ah, but no procession would be complete without the
accompaniment of happy island song!"

And, of course, the song began:

> "Now we're going on a trip,
>   Wakka Heenie, Wakka Ho.
> But not by air and not by ship,

Wakka Heenie, Wakka Ho.
So we approach on dancing feet,
Wakka Heenie, Wakka Ho.
'Cause Wakka Loa's gotta eat!
Wakka Heenie, *Unnhhh*!"

No! Roger tried to close his ears to the music. He would
not fall under the insidious island spell again. He felt the
jacket pocket of his jogging suit. Yes, the ring was still
there! If he could reach Delores, and if he could somehow
get Doc and Louie to join them, he'd get all four of them
out of this place faster than you could say "See you in the
funny papers!"

Well, there was Zabana too. Roger would have to figure
out some way to rescue the jungle prince as well, but at
least the blond giant was out of immediate danger. He'd
worry about all these things once he'd reached Delores.

If he could reach her. A pair of burly islanders hustled
her forward, up the ever-increasing slope. Still, if he
sprinted, he should be able to catch them. Shouldn't he?

He looked down at his feet. They were no longer running, but walking forward in a very deliberate rhythm.
Step. Step. Hop, hop, hop. Step. Step. Hop, hop, hop.
One, two. One, two, three. Roger realized they were moving in time with the music.

"Second verse!" the elder called.

And the islanders replied:

"Oh, this trip will be a gas,
Wakka Heenie, Wakka Ho;
'Cause for some, this trip's the last,
Wakka Heenie, Wakka Ho.
In this regard I've got a hunch,
Wakka Heenie, Wakka Ho;
'Cause Wakka Loa needs its lunch!
Wakka Heenie, *Unnnhhhh*!"

One, two. One, two, three. Step. Step. Hop, hop, hop.
Roger had never realized dancing could be so fulfilling.
He'd reach Delores sooner or later. Now, dancing was his

life. One, two. One, two, three. Step. Step. Hop, hop—

Wait a second. Roger blinked, trying to concentrate. He had to reach Delores. He had to use the ring. He had to get out of here, or he was going to be sacrificed to a volcano god. One, two. One, two, three. It was all so hard to remember when you had dancing feet.

Roger glanced around and saw that everyone else in the procession was also dancing their way up the mountainside. One, two. One, two, three. And well they should. Step. Step. Hop, hop, hop. He threw his head to the sky, thrusting his arms and shoulders forward to the relentless beat. He was really dancing now!

"Third verse!" the elder called.

About time, Roger thought. It was too late to stop now.

> "Oh it's truly time for action,
> Wakka Heenie, Wakka Ho.
> Let's give volcano satisfaction,
> Wakka Heenie, Wakka Ho.
> For when we give the god its measure,
> Wakka Heenie, Wakka Ho;
> Wakka Loa burps with pleasure!
> Wakka Heenie, *Unnnnnhhhhhhh*!"

One, two. One, two, three. One, two. One, two, three. His legs leapt up the hill in time to the music. What could be better than this? Roger looked up the path and saw the first puffs of dark, volcanic smoke drift by above. The thought filled his head suddenly. Roger laughed at how obvious it was. One, two. One, two, three. And how wonderful! After dancing like this—one, two—there was only one thing that could be better—one, two, three—being sacrificed to a volcano god!

Roger couldn't wait. At last, the answer to all his dancing dreams. To be sacrificed to Wakka Loa—already, he could hear the BOOM *Boom* Boom boom of the drums in his head. Nothing could stop him now. Unless—

Roger looked down at his clothes with some distress. His shiny blue jogging suit wasn't all that shiny anymore.

The fabric was covered by layers of Western dust, and the fabric had been torn in three or four places by jungle undergrowth. Roger frowned. He looked rather more disheveled than he would have wished. One, two. One, two, three. What if he had come all this way, and the Volcano God didn't want him? That couldn't happen, could it? After all, he was dancing up this hill for the express purpose of becoming volcano fodder. But what if Wakka Loa was a stickler for sacrificial hygiene? Roger got so upset, he almost stopped dancing.

There had to be something he could do to keep from getting rejected. One, two. One, two, three. Wasn't there some way he could make up for his somewhat less than pristine condition?

The thought hit him faster than his feet could fly. What he needed was a garnish! Surely the Volcano God could never reject him if he came specially prepared—particularly if he were wearing complementary foodstuffs. As Roger saw it, all they ever seemed to do around this island was eat and dance, anyway. Surely somebody in this procession would be carrying something appropriate.

"Anybody got a pineapple ring or two?" he called out to the surrounding dancers. "Some carrot sticks?"

The island women smiled as they cha-cha-ed by.

"A candied apple?" he asked an island warrior, desperation in his voice. The warrior executed a particularly complicated rhumba step.

He turned back to Big Louie and Doc, who followed close behind. His voice was hoarse with urgency: "A little parsley for color?"

But Louie seemed busy with the fox trot, and Doc looked like he was dosey-do-ing.

No one heard him. They were too busy dancing. A garnish was out of the question. He would never transcend his dirty, ragged self.

He was so upset, he almost tripped. His feet weren't even moving right. He stopped dead.

He blinked.

What was he doing?

Not only was he going to get sacrificed—willingly—to a volcano god, he had been planning on adding personal decoration so that the sacrifice would occur. How crazy was he?

Only as crazy, Roger realized with a chill, as the music had made him. Now that he had regained his sanity, he had to get out of here, fast. He realized now that the song the islanders sang enslaved him, and made him so pliant to their will that he was coming up with extra ways to ensure his demise. Only if he got away from the music could he discover some way of rescuing Delores and the others. Only if he could keep from dancing could he stay free of the island's spells.

"Last verse!" the elder screamed.

Roger turned to run. One step, two steps. One, two, three steps. His feet turned back the other way.

> "Hey now, it's no time to stop,
> Wakka Heenie, Wakka Ho;
> For we have almost reached the top.
> Wakka Heenie, Wakka Ho.
> No dawdling there, in front or back,
> Wakka Heenie, Wakka Ho;
> 'Cause you're a Wakka Loa snack!
> Wakka Heenie, *Unnnnhhhhhh!*"

What had Roger been so upset about? He couldn't remember. How could anybody be upset when they could dance? One, two. One, two, three.

The dancers rounded a bend in the steep moutainside path. The way leveled off ahead, and broadened into a sort of natural shelf. The islander's festive sarongs looked especially striking against the black of the pumice up here, a warehouse-long floor of stone unbroken by vegetation. Roger glanced to his right. There was a thousand-foot drop, straight to the ocean's crashing surf.

To his left was the lip of the volcano, close enough that he might reach it if he stood on tiptoe. Roger nodded his agreement as he danced. Not only was this shelf very attractive, it was convenient, too.

"And now we come to the end of our journey," the elder intoned, "the place where our cheerful islanders practice the most ancient of their quaint native customs!"

Roger joined the cheerful islanders as they shouted back: "Wakka Loa!"

BOOM *Boom* Boom boom, the drums replied as usual. Somehow, they sounded closer to Roger, but perhaps it was only the clear mountain air.

"But that's not all!" the elder continued. "The happy natives have reserved a special place of honor for their visitors!" He pointed to four stone slabs at the very center of the plateau.

One, two. One, two, three. Roger cha-cha-ed toward the nearest slab. It was made of dark volcanic rock as well, but the rock had been polished and slightly curved to better accommodate a human form. Roger smiled. What a comfortable-looking sacrificial table. And they had placed drainage holes in the center of the slab, as well—so that the blood could pour away neatly, without the mess. How considerate these locals were. How lucky he was to be involved in a really first-class sacrifice!

He was aware of others around him. Doc and Big Louie cha-cha-ed to his left. And on his right? Delores' deep blue eyes looked into his own.

His feet stopped dead again.

Delores was going to be sacrificed! And almost as bad, he was going to be sacrificed, too! Even worse than that, before he saw Delores, he would have willingly climbed up on that table and pointed straight to his heart with a cheerful "Stick the knife here." The music spell had been that strong.

But, one look in those wondrous blue eyes, and he was his own man. His feelings for Delores were stronger than any Movie Magic the Cineverse could throw at him.

"Oh, Roger," Delores whispered to him. "Why didn't you get away while you had the chance?"

"But, Delores," Roger replied rapidly, "we're free of

their spell now. We still have that chance—"

That's when two burly islanders grabbed him from behind. Roger never did figure out where they got the rope. He didn't get any chance to ask, either, before he was thrown up on the sacrificial table and tied securely.

"And now," the elder announced, "the islanders all wait for the appearance of their leader so that this colorful ceremony may begin!"

"Oh, Roger," Delores moaned softly from the next table, where she was similarly trussed. "Why did I get you into this?"

Roger smiled reassuringly at her. "Hey, nobody forced me—"

Her voice hushed but urgent, Delores interrupted before he could even finish his gallant retort. "Oh, but I did, in my way. Cineverse knows you never would have met Doctor Dread or Big Louie if it hadn't been for me. And you wouldn't have known about the ring's true purpose, or anything about a place that has volcano god sacrifices—there's so much I'm responsible for! That's why I tried to keep you from coming out to save me when I was tied to the tree."

"Oh, yes," Roger replied, not quite knowing what else to say. "That."

"I had to do something!" Delores pleaded. "They said they'd kill me if I told you about the traps. How can I explain? You see, they needed someone to sacrifice to the Volcano God. Well, they already had their standard sacrifices, but apparently the god found a constant meal plan of island virgins tedious. The volcano was grumbling. They were afraid it might erupt unless something was done. At least that's what the Lord Fufu claimed. They decided that Wakka Loa—"

BOOM *Boom* Boom boom, the drums interrupted.

"—needed some variety in its diet," Delores concluded. "That variety is me and you."

"Oh," Roger replied again. Why was it that whenever Delores explained anything about the Cineverse, Roger felt more confused than he had before?

"Well, originally," Delores continued, "it was only going to be you. You and your companions, that is. Doctor Dread arranged for you to be taken, and put out of the way, as he phrased it. And the obvious bait to trap you with was me." She briefly flashed her fabulous smile. "And so they tied me to that tree, with strict instructions that I wasn't to tell you about the large pits that surrounded me, or the dozen muscular islanders ready to set upon you with clubs and other dull instruments as soon as you entered the clearing." She sighed. "And if I disobeyed, if I told you anything about the danger, I was to be sacrificed with you!"

"Oh, Delores!" Roger whispered, truly understanding at last.

"So it was that I was forbidden to warn you," she continued. "However, they hadn't forbidden me from sending you away by other means. What could I do, then, but spurn you?" She turned away from him then, looking up at the wisps of smoke that drifted down from the volcano. "It was the only way I could save the man I loved!"

Roger's heart pounded against his rib cage. How could he have been such a fool? How could he have doubted her for a minute? If only he wasn't tied up here, he would— but he was very securely tied, and about to become volcano fodder! He took a deep breath, bringing his emotions under control as he realized that, even after all her explanations, there was still a thing or two he didn't understand.

"But—if you didn't disobey their instructions—why are you here?"

"Oh," she answered, turning back to him. "They didn't like me sending you away much, either. So they decided to sacrifice me to the Volcano God, after all."

"Actually, I have another question," Roger added. "Who exactly is 'they'?"

"Why, Doctor Dread and his henchpeople, of course. That's how I know about all these things. Dread likes to talk. He doesn't necessarily want to say anything, but he can spend hours implying, if you know what I mean. It's even worse than I thought." Her voice dropped to an even lower whisper. "It's rumored the Plotmaster's dead."

Roger stared at her. Maybe somebody could finally tell him about the Plotmaster.

"The Plotmaster?" Louie blurted from where he was tied to the next slab over. "Dead?"

Delores grimaced. "Your friend here has awfully acute hearing."

"Yeah," Roger agreed somewhat distractedly, "or something." He struggled to find the words. "But, the Plotmaster—"

Louie laughed in disbelief. "Well, let's face it, with the way things are going around here, he had to be sick, or at least on vacation. But dead?"

"No, no, he's not dead!" Roger cried fervently. He saw a figure standing in his memory; a figure surrounded by light, and wisps of blue smoke rising from a cigar.

"But who is—?" Roger started again.

This time he was interrupted by the rumble of the volcano, deep below the sacrificial tables.

"And now," the elder announced all over again, "the islanders all wait for the appearance of their leader so that this colorful ceremony may begin!"

"Yeah!" Louie agreed, fidgeting about on his stone slab. "I mean, shouldn't we be sacrificed by now?"

"Louie!" Roger yelled, realizing it still wasn't time to worry about the Plotmaster. What was the sidekick saying?

But the sidekick was adamant. "Back in Brooklyn, when you wanted somethin' done, it got done. I mean, look at us! It gets uncomfortable, tied up like this. You can't scratch where it itches."

"Louie—" Roger began again, but could think of nothing coherent to follow it with. Louie must still be under the island's insidious musical spell.

"Hey!" Louie explained. "The least a victim can expect is a little service."

"No, your small friend is correct," the elder reticently agreed. "The ceremony should be swift and sure, not to mention as dramatic as all get out. It is a Law of the Islands. Still, we await the legendary Lord Fufu!"

The volcano rumbled again. A great plume of dense smoke rose above their heads.

The elder's perpetual smile faltered. "Then again, if we must wait much longer, Wakka Loa—"

BOOM *Boom* Boom boom.

"—may make this wait our last," he concluded.

"Hey!" Louie continued, adamant. "If we have to keep on waiting, the least you can do is untie my hands so I can get in a final scratch."

The elder looked meaningfully at the two islanders who stood like statues to either side of Louie's slab. One of the men moved his hands ever so slightly so that it rested against the large knife strapped to his thigh.

"Don't like that idea, huh?" The small man squirmed uncomfortably on the stone table. "Well, what the hey—I'm easygoing. What say you just untie *one* of my hands?"

The frowning islander with the knife pulled it free of its sheath and held it over Louie's heart.

"Unfortunately, that cannot be allowed," the elder replied, still somewhat distracted. "As much as they wish to please their visitors, the natives will allow no interference with their quaint and picturesque customs."

"No problem," Louie agreed. "Just asking. Hey, we're all friends here, right?"

The islander, still scowling, replaced the knife in its sheath.

Louie smiled and shrugged at Roger. "The least a sidekick can do is try."

Roger nodded back, a little shaken as he realized Louie had been trying to escape. Instead, they had come awfully close to pathos.

And, in a minute, if Roger didn't come up with something, it would be pathos for everybody.

The ground shook beneath them as the volcano rumbled again. The crowd around him gasped.

"Wakka Loa!"

Roger looked to where the crowd pointed as the drumbeats faded away.

A crack had formed in the volcano wall. It wasn't very wide or very long, but there was steam coming from it.

"And now," the elder announced with a certain amount of panic in his voice, "the islanders all wait—not to mention pray—for the very rapid appearance of their leader so that this colorful ceremony may begin without further delay!"

"All right, already!" a voice boomed from the usual explosion of blue smoke. "Somebody did something with my island high-priest sacrificing costume! I had to find something else"—the voice paused significantly—"appropriate."

Roger already knew who it was before the smoke cleared. Only one man could make silence so insidious. However, it was only after the island breezes had blown the blue haze away again that he saw Doctor Dread was wearing his black and red wizard's costume.

Doctor Dread glanced over at Roger. He smiled as the islander next to Louie handed him that knife. The villain chuckled.

"Now," he continued in that oily way he had, "I believe it's time for a little"—he hesitated suggestively—"ceremony?"

CHAPTER
23

"And now," the elder said with finality, "our visitors bid a fond farewell to this peaceful island. They know, no matter where they travel, they'll never forget our paradise under the sun!"

Doctor Dread walked toward Roger, the very large, very sharp, extremely pointed knife in his upraised hand. Somehow, though, Roger couldn't keep his eyes off the strange blood-red runes upon Dread's costume, which, once again, seemed to spell out arcane—yet strangely familiar—messages; things that somehow hinted at a deeper meaning. Roger squinted, barely making out the words:

BORN . . . Roger read slowly . . . FOR FUN, LOYAL . . . TO NONE

There was a muttering among the islanders. Far away, Roger heard the volcano grumble.

"Now," Dread announced to the assemblage, "the ceremony begins!"

But before he could reach Roger's slab, another of the islanders stepped in his path. This new fellow spoke quickly as he stared at the ground.

"Begging your pardon, O great Lord Fufu. But you are not wearing the traditional costume of sacrifice."

"What?" Dread exploded. "You dare to question the great Lord Fufu? Haven't I explained my"—he hesitated knowingly—"problems to you? The costume has been"—he paused tellingly—"misplaced."

But the islander did not move. "I felt someone should mention it. Perhaps the ceremony should not take place. We do not want to offend Wakka Loa. What if the volcano doesn't recognize you?"

Dread/Fufu laughed. "Of course it shall recognize me. Am I not the volcano's"—he stopped meaningfully—"servant? Now, out of my way. There are those who must be" —he delayed even more purposefully, his eyes wandering to the rows of sacrificial tables—"dealt with."

The islander obsequiously shuffled aside, and Dread quickly covered the last few steps to Roger's slab. He leaned close to his intended victim, his smile dazzling in the island sunshine. Unfortunately for his victim-to-be, he had obviously eaten something with garlic for lunch. Still, Roger could not look away. The runes on his wizard's hat danced before Roger's eyes:

I'M . . . WITH . . . STUPID

Dread lifted the dagger even higher, so that it shone in the perpetual sunshine. Roger wondered if he should close his eyes, but decided he might as well see the last moment of his life.

Dread chuckled triumphantly. "Now, I shall"—he paused ceremonially—"take care of this sacrifice, in the name of Wakka Loa!"

He waited, knife in the air, for the answering beat. But there was nothing. No drums, no sound beyond the island wind. The islanders looked uneasily at their high priest.

"Wakka Loa!" Dread yelled again.

One more moment of silence. Then the volcano rumbled.

Some of the islanders screamed.

"Wakka Loa!" Dread screamed in desperation.

He was answered this time, not by drums, but by a deep voice:

"Will not be answered by volcano! Will be answered by Zabana!"

The jungle prince ran into view upon the mountain path.

"Bunga bonga blooie! Aieeaieeooo!"

"How dare you!" the wizard-suited high priest screamed. Dread turned to face the jungle prince. Roger turned his head to follow the action. The runes upon the back of Dread's flowing costume formed the most complex message of all:

MY PARENTS WENT TO . . . CAMELOT, AND ALL I GOT WERE . . . THESE LOUSY WIZARD'S ROBES!"

"Zabana dares all!" the jungle prince replied. "I will call upon my island friends to free your prisoners. Come, O wild pigs of the island. Stampede up mountain! Save Zabana's friends!" He cupped his hands around his mouth as he called: "Oink, oink! Wagawaga! Gruum!"

He looked about expectantly, but, this time, it was Zabana who was answered by silence.

"Our newest visitor learns another secret of our tiny paradise," the elder explained. "For, peaceful as it is in our perfect kingdom, all our pigs recently expired from an outbreak of swine flu. Unfortunately, we must import all our wild pigs from the next island over."

"I think our newcomer will fit in nicely in the sacrifice's second shift," Doctor Dread suggested. He nodded at those already tied up on the slabs. "Four tables. No waiting."

The jungle prince got a particularly wild look in his eyes. "Zabana try again! Call upon wild jungle monkey! Come, Zabana's allies! Chatter and swing and overrun this place! Save Zabana's friends!" He cupped his hands to his mouth once more. "Chee Chee! Ooga Ooga! Gruum!"

He waited, muscles tense. There was no more noise than the first time.

"Alas," the elder commented softly, "our newest visitor has discovered yet another island tragedy. For all the cute and furry denizens of our paradise upon the sea have succumbed to a wild outbreak of monkey fever, and are no more. We have thought of importing some from the next island, but have, until now, been too busy with our quaint island ceremonies."

But his newest failure seemed only to steel the jungle prince's resolve. "Zabana not defeated! Zabana never defeated! Zabana use something he know is here!" The jungle prince paused a moment in thought. "Call upon wild jungle parrot! Fly to volcano! Flutter! Peck! Disrupt! Save Zabana's friends!" His hands once again to his mouth, his cry reverberated through the air: "Squawk squawk glizzard! Polly want a cracker! Gluum!"

This time, there was a response. Roger heard the sound of a thousand wings and, a moment later, saw what looked like a blanket of a hundred different colors flying up the volcano trail from the jungle below. But as the blanket drew ever closer, he realized it was really innumerable parrots flying in impossibly close formation, their uncountable wings beating furiously in answer to Zabana's call.

"Zabana triumphs!" the jungle prince called. "Bunga bonga blooie! Aieeeaieeeoooo!"

With that, the parrots descended. Thousands of cries of "Polly want a cracker" and "Who's the pretty boy?" filled the air.

Somehow, in the ensuing confusion, Roger realized that the blond giant had reached his side and, what's more, he had brought a friend. The newcomer was another islander, although he appeared to be more bronzed and athletically built than any of the other incredibly well-muscled fellows Roger had already seen hereabouts.

The jungle prince smiled. "Zabana bring reinforcements!"

"Reinforcements?" Roger asked before he could stop himself. "From where?"

"Zabana explore island," the jungle prince explained. "Zabana find drummer."

The tall bronzed figure nodded solemnly. "I have put away my drums. The jungle prince has convinced me that we are all a party to injustice."

"Stay still," the jungle prince told Roger. "Zabana free

you." With both of his massive hands he grabbed the thick coconut rope that crisscrossed Roger's chest. His arm muscles bulged. He gritted his teeth. A single drop of sweat rolled from his forehead.

Zabana pulled. The rope disintegrated in his hands like dental floss.

"Zabana triumphs! Bunga bonga blooie!"

He moved quickly, freeing Delores in much the same way.

"Excuse me," she asked, pointing to Zabana's belt. "Not to seem ungrateful or anything, but couldn't you have used the knife?"

"Knife?" Zabana frowned down at his belt as if he had never seen a knife before. "Much more satisfying to rip and tear. Properly dramatic for jungle prince."

Roger sat up, massaging the rope burns on his arms and ankles. He looked around as the drummer—not afraid to use his own knife—cut Doc free of his ropes. Roger congratulated their newest ally on his decision.

The drummer shrugged. "Well, perhaps I had some ulterior motive. Do you know how boring it is to go BOOM *Boom* Boom boom all day?"

"Hey, I can understand that," Louie agreed as Zabana shredded his ropes. "I used to be in comedy relief."

Beyond their own little drama, Roger noticed that the parrot attack had not had quite the chaotic effect Zabana had originally hoped. He quickly pointed this out to the jungle hero.

"Parrots not particularly good fighters," Zabana admitted. "Offer them cracker, they go over to the other side."

But there seemed to be more wrong here than a simple case of bird allegiance. Some of the nearby parrots looked awfully motley, as if they were losing their feathers. Still others seemed to be having trouble with their voices:

"Who's the pretty—?" Cough.

"Polly want a—" Hack, hack.

"Hey!" Roger exclaimed. "These parrots are sick!"

Zabana nodded. "Like wild pigs. Like monkeys. Wild parrot whooping cough."

"But what would make all these animals sick?" Roger frowned, not wishing to believe the next thought that entered his mind. "There couldn't be something to this Volcano God curse, could there?"

"Hey, you know," Louie replied. "Why do they call it Movie Magic?"

The ground shook beneath their feet.

"Wakka Loa!" the islanders screamed in fear.

"BOOM *Boom* Boom boom," the drummer remarked. He glanced at Roger. "Sorry. Old habits."

Roger replied with another sticky question. "But that means the volcano—deprived of its sacrifice—is actually going to erupt?"

"Suddenly, the visitors realize what they have done to our sultry island paradise." The elder looked directly at Roger. "You have angered Wakka Loa. Now the volcano will eat all of us!"

"Hey," Louie replied, "what would a South Sea Island Paradise be without a few falling rocks and some dramatic white-hot lava?"

"Unfortunately," Doctor Dread screamed, "you will not live long enough to find out! To me, my minions!"

A group clad in traditional native dress charged through the remaining chaos, ignoring their fellows' troubles with whatever parrots remained. Roger frowned. Something seemed wrong here. These newcomers were awfully pale for islanders. Plus, Roger hadn't—at least until he saw this group—noticed any of the locals sporting pencil-thin mustaches. And then there was that very tall woman in the back, wearing a sarong that looked like nothing so much as a modified pup tent—that is, if they designed pup tents in floral island colors. But it was the way this woman stared at Roger that he found truly disquieting. It was a definite Big Bertha stare.

The earth shivered beneath his feet. The last of the parrots flew away as many of the real islanders began to run down the path to the jungle below. Roger saw that Dread's band had somehow produced guns, blackjacks, and brass knuckles from somewhere beneath their grass skirts. They laughed evilly as they approached Roger and his companions.

"What do we do now?" Louie asked no one in particular.

Delores clutched Roger's hand. "Whatever happens," she whispered in his ear, "it will happen to us together!"

"Zabana!" Roger called to the blond giant by his side. "Can't you do something?"

But the large fellow only frowned. "What can Zabana call? Monkey's gone! Pigs gone! Parrots going! Zabana out of animals! Jungle prince have to think!"

Zabana had to think? Then perhaps they were truly lost.

"Excellent!" Doctor Dread chortled. "They have been a thorn in my side for far too long! They are defenseless. Deal with them now!"

"Ah, but we are not defenseless!" the drummer declared. "Hope is never lost when you still have your drums!"

Roger turned back to their newest ally and noticed that he now stood behind a pair of waist-high conga drums. Roger was too confused by now to even wonder where they had come from.

Rumble, rumble, went the volcano.

BOOM *Boom* Boom boom, replied the drummer.

But Dread only laughed. "You expect to stop us with some pitiful musical instrument?"

Boom BOOM *Boom* boom, was the drummer's only reply.

Dread waved his henchpeople forward. "Attend to them!"

Boom boom BOOM *Boom*, the drummer answered smartly.

And the volcano seemed to rumble again in reply. This whole exchange certainly was rhythmic. Roger hoped it meant something too.

"Usher them out!" Dread shrieked as his henchpeople lumbered forward.

That's when the ground beneath them shook with a force so great it threatened to knock Roger and his fellows off their feet. The minions hesitated in their deadly charge.

Only the drummer seemed unaffected, keeping up his steady beat.

"Subtract them from the ledger!" Dread screamed as he threw his wizard's cap to the ground.

BOOM *Boom* BOOM Boom *Boom* boom BOOM, the drummer responded. And the volcano responded as well.

It started out as a crack on the incline behind Dread and his cronies. But before the gang had taken another step, it had widened to a fissure that glowed red from deep within. The volcano rumbled, and the fissure rippled forward with the speed of a tidal wave obliterating a beach.

The evildoers screamed in unison as the chasm opened beneath them.

"Give my regards to Wakka Loa!" Louie yelled as they disappeared from sight.

The rumbling stopped. The fissure no longer grew. The volcano made one final noise, accompanied by a great cloud of gray ash. It sounded like nothing so much as a colossal belch.

"Wakka Loa accepts the sacrifice," the elder remarked from nearby, where, Roger was surprised to note, he still stood.

Then all was quiet.

"One is never defenseless," their savior repeated, "when one has drums."

So the drummer had rescued them, and satiated the Volcano God at the same time. Roger was incredibly relieved.

"How can we ever thank you?" he asked.

But the tall islander brushed Roger's question aside with a wave of his hand. "No thanks are necessary. And remember—never sleep in a wet canoe!"

After a reminder like that, Roger wasn't at all surprised when the drummer disappeared in a cloud of blue smoke.

"Was that—?" Roger began.

"I plumb reckon—" Doc added.

"Do you mean—?" Big Louie continued.

"Ah," the island elder called from where he still stood behind them. "Then you did not recognize him? Come now. Even though you are visitors to our island paradise, surely you've heard of the Secret Samoan."

Oh, no. The Secret Samoan? Roger couldn't believe it. They had missed Captain Crusader again!

"Do not look so distraught, my love," Delores chided.

"But Captain Crusader—"

She kissed him gently on the cheek. "So you missed the hero's hero? Is that so bad, now? Aren't we together at last? And haven't we dealt with the biggest threat Captain Crusader had? I mean, with the way things are now, we have all the time in the Cineverse to find him." She nudged Roger suggestively. "And perhaps we'll have time for a few other things as well."

"She's right!" Big Louie grinned. "With Dread out of the way, what could possibly go wrong now?"

"But perhaps our visitors speak too soon," the elder intoned, "for there are always surprises aplenty in this island paradise." He casually pointed at the hand that had appeared on the lip of the fissure.

It was followed by a foot, some six feet away. An ash-covered figure pulled itself from the chasm. Roger shuddered when he saw the figure was wearing a somewhat singed floral pup tent.

"You have not escaped me yet," Big Bertha announced as she dragged someone else from the pit with her other hand, a man wearing the tattered remains of a wizard's robes.

Dread glared at Roger and the others as he regained his footing. "*Us*, my dear woman. They have not escaped"— he paused significantly—"us."

But Zabana stepped forward. "Jungle prince laughs at danger! What threat are ash-covered villains? They are defenseless against might of Zabana!"

"Well, not exactly defenseless." Big Bertha whipped a machine gun from within the folds of her dress. She smiled triumphantly. "It's amazing how many weapons you can hide inside a sarong."

"Deal with them slowly," Dread suggested.

"Yesss," Bertha hissed, her eyes darting up and down

Roger's jogging-suited form. "And I know which one I shall deal with last."

"Quick!" Louie shouted. "The ring!"

For once, Big Louie was right. Roger pulled the Captain Crusader Decoder Ring from his jacket pocket.

"Where do I set it?" he asked frantically.

"Oh, no you don't!" Bertha pointed her machine gun at Roger.

"If only I had my six-guns!" Doc shot back. "Or my guitar!"

"If only Zabana had animals!" the jungle prince raged.

"Deal with them!" Dread shrieked as he leapt up and down. "Take care of them! Oh—in the name of all that is evil—shoot them!"

Louie grabbed for the ring. "Here, let me set it!"

Roger felt the tiny circle of plastic yanked from his grasp.

A single shot rang out.

"Roger!" Delores screamed.

But Roger was surrounded by blue smoke, the only sound the fading words of the village elder:

"Whenever our visitors must leave our island paradise, they always feel it is too soon. . . ."

After that, all was darkness.

CHAPTER

⌒ 24 ⌒

Roger woke up in bed. His bed. Back where he had started from. On Earth. Out of the Cineverse. Only worse. Now he was all alone.

He tried to remember what had happened. The last thing he could recall was being threatened by a besmirched Big Bertha toting a machine gun. Well, that, and big Louie grabbing the Captain Crusader Decoder Ring as a shot rang out.

A gunshot? Roger looked down at the dirty, torn jogging suit he still wore. No, there didn't seem to be any new hole. As far as he could tell, he was still intact. The bullet must have gone somewhere else.

But there was something else that was very wrong.

The Captain Crusader Decoder Ring! Even before he reached into his pocket, Roger knew it was gone. Louie had grabbed it, after all. Roger had felt it slip out of his fingers at the exact same instant the shot rang out and the blue smoke appeared. He wondered if there was some pattern to all of that. Obviously, the ring had worked somehow. Otherwise, he wouldn't be back here. Far away from

Delores and the rest of his companions, who at this very instant were being menaced, if not shot, by Doctor Dread and Big Bertha.

He had no ring! What could he do? Well, he wouldn't panic. He had found that first ring easily enough—and, even with his mother's wholesale selling of his possessions, there were still enough boxes to go through so that there had to be another ring in there somewhere.

Roger pushed the rumpled sheets aside and got out of bed. Obviously, it was time to visit his mother.

First, however, he should change his jogging suit. It wouldn't do to be seen in the streets wearing the rags he had on now. And he should take a shower, too. He had to look presentable if he was going to get into his mother's basement.

He glanced at the clock. The digital dial said 9:15. He looked at the window and saw light seeping through the venetian blinds. So that would make it 9:15 in the morning. But which morning? Roger had no idea how long he had been in the Cineverse. It might have been hours, it might have been days. Still, what did it matter? His mother was home most mornings. This would be a good time to call.

She picked up at the end of the first ring.

"Hi, Mom!" he said brightly, wanting to make this whole thing as short as possible.

"Roger?" his mother's voice replied in disbelief. "Where have you been?"

"Been?" Roger replied defensively, surprised at the vehemence of his mother's reaction. It was amazing how few words it took for her to make him feel like a guilty twelve-year-old. "Well, you know. Here and there."

His response seemed to upset her even more. "Here and there? You've been missing for two weeks, and that's where you've been—*here and there*? I tell you, when Susan called me after she couldn't find you, I was beside myself with worry. Thank goodness that dear Mr. Mengeles is so easy to talk to. I'll have you know he's had to calm me down more than once. Otherwise, I don't know what I would have done!"

"Two weeks?" Roger replied. How could he have been gone for two weeks? Was time in the Cineverse different from that in Boston? And what was Susan doing, butting into his business again, anyway?

"About Susan—" Roger continued.

"She's such a dear girl," his mother agreed. "I don't see why you ignore her so."

"Mother! She's the one who divorced me!"

"Just because she ran off with that grocer?" his mother chided. "You've let that blind you to all her positive qualities."

Positive qualities? Roger decided to give up on the argument. He couldn't think of any woman he had been involved with—and Roger had to admit that covered a lot of territory—who had less "positive" associated with her than Susan. Well, there had been Debbie, he supposed, but that was at least in part because of her snake collection. Discounting such outside circumstance, Susan had the market cornered on negative associations.

Besides, Roger realized, whatever Susan wanted really didn't matter anymore. When he thought about it rationally—something he had always had trouble with when it came to Susan—all he really had to do was fetch another one of his rings and he was out of there. He had a whole new Cineverse waiting for him—a Cineverse that was miraculously Susan-free.

"Look, Mom," he said with finality. "We can talk about Susan some other time. I need to look through my things again. Maybe I'll even move them out. You've had to store them long enough."

"Why, that's very nice of you, dear," his mother said, surprised. "But dear Mr. Mengeles—"

Roger wouldn't be sidetracked again. He interrupted before his mother could go off on another tangent:

"That's nice. Will you be home today?"

"Why, yes. At least until four. That's when I have to go pick—"

"I'll be over in an hour," Roger said. He hung up the phone and walked into the bathroom to take a shower. He had to hurry, to get past his mother and all her stories of Mr. Mengeles and Roger's ex-wives and whatever else popped into her head. Anything could be happening in the Cineverse. Anything. And he couldn't bear to think he had finally found Delores, only to lose her forever.

He made it to his mother's house in forty-five minutes.

"Roger? You're early? But you're never early!"

He kissed her on the cheek as he stepped inside the house. "Sorry, Mom. Don't have time to talk. I'll just go down and fetch my stuff."

"Roger?" Her voice followed him down the stairs. "But Roger—"

"I'll talk to you in a minute, Mom!" He ran his hand along the wall. If Mr. Mengeles was so handy, he should have installed a light switch to go along with the new rec room. Ah, there it was. "I've got to start hauling this stuff up!"

Now, where had they put that storage closet? Roger spotted it on the far side of the room. He heard his mother coming down the stairs. She just didn't want to leave him alone, did she? Well, he was going to do this quickly, one way or another. He walked swiftly across the new linoleum and opened the door. It was dark inside. Wasn't there an overhead pull-light in here?

"Roger!" his mother reprimanded as she reached the bottom of the stairs. "I'm trying to tell you something!"

"Sure, Mom. In a minute." Roger groped in the closet's dark upper reaches, searching for a hanging bit of string. He felt something brush the back of his knuckles. Paydirt.

"You will do just what you want, won't you?" His mother sighed. "You were always such a willful boy."

"In a second, Mother," Roger repeated, more from habit than from thought. He pulled the string.

The light went on, illuminating the remaining storage space.

The closet was empty.

"My stuff!" Roger yelled, spinning to face his mother. "It's gone!"

"Well, what did you think I was trying to tell you?" She tapped her foot in that all-suffering way she had.

But Roger was in no mood for suffering. "Where is it? What have you done with it?"

His mother took a half step backward. "Roger. Please don't raise your voice. Think of the neighbors. Your things are perfectly safe. Mr. Mengeles has simply moved them to the garage."

"The garage?" Roger rushed past her, taking the steps two at a time. There was something about finding that closet empty—All his confidence had evaporated. What if the other Captain Crusader Decoder Rings were gone? What if his mother had gotten rid of the rest of them a long time ago? What if he could never find his way to the Cineverse again? He had been anxious to find the rings before; now he was desperate.

His mother followed him up the stairs. She could move with surprising speed when she wanted to.

Someone rang the frong doorbell. His mother hustled by him to answer it.

A familiar baldheaded gentleman stood on the front step.

"Why, Mr. M!" his mother gushed in a much more girlish voice than she ever used with Roger. "What a surprise!"

Mengeles frowned as he shook his head thoughtfully. "I heard voices over here, Mrs. G. Raised voices. Thought I'd just look in and make sure everything was all right."

"How thoughtful of you, Mr. M!" She impulsively grabbed the older man's arm. "It was only Roger, I'm afraid. He got a little upset that we'd moved his things. You know the way that children are."

"Indeed I do, Mrs. G." He waved past her at her son. "Nice to see you again, Roger. Well, perhaps I should be going."

But Mother, with her grip firmly established, wasn't about to let go. "Certainly not, Mr. M! You came over here because you were concerned about my safety. The least I can do is reward you with a cup of coffee!"

Mengeles relented with the slight smile of one who knows he's been outmatched. "Oh, very well, Mrs. G. While you're doing that, what say Roger and I go to the garage? I'll show him where we've put his things."

She let go of him to clap her hands. "Oh, you're such a thoughtful man! Isn't he, Roger?"

Roger nodded, wondering how he could get rid of this fellow. He certainly didn't want anybody else seeing the Captain Crusader Decoder Rings. He didn't want to have to explain anything to any overaged Romeo his mother had—

Roger stopped himself. What was he thinking? How could anyone around here know the significance of a Captain Crusader Decoder Ring? And, even if they did, how would you explain the Cineverse to them? Nobody would believe it. Now that he was back on Earth, there was a part of Roger that didn't want to believe it either.

"Okay," he said to Mengeles. "Lead on."

The older man did just that, leading Roger through the kitchen to the back door. Mother waved as she put the coffeepot on the stove. Roger followed Mengeles down the concrete steps into the garage.

"We put all your stuff on the shelves in the back here. You were so upset last time you came to visit your mother, she figured you'd probably be better off if you just took your things and stored them yourself. That's why we brought everything up here—so it would be easier for you to get at."

"Sure, sure," Roger replied, only half listening. Mengeles seemed as good as his mother at long-winded explanations. He hurried over to the pile of boxes that held the remains of his childhood.

"Of course, there is one other thing," the older man added as Roger walked away. He reached up and shut the door. "You will permit me to gloat. I've waited so long for this moment."

There was something so odd in the older man's tone that Roger paused and looked around.

"How shall I put this?" Mengeles asked, obviously pleased with Roger's attention. "How about this? I wouldn't bother wasting my time looking for Captain Crusader Decoder Rings."

Roger's mouth fell open.

"Oh, you shouldn't be surprised," Mengeles continued smoothly. "Doctor Dread likes to think of everything." He reached into his pocket. "You had four more of them, you know." Roger heard the clack of plastic on plastic. "In very good condition, too. Ready to be used by someone more" —he paused significantly—"deserving than yourself."

"What?" Roger demanded. "You can't do this!"

"Who's going to stop me?" Mengeles purred.

Roger started toward the steps. "I'm going in to tell my mother!"

His threat didn't faze Mengeles in the least. "And what will you tell her? Think about it. We're talking about the Cineverse here, a bunch of crazy movie worlds that you travel between, using a cheap plastic ring. How are you going to explain that? And, even if you somehow managed an explanation, do you think your mother would believe you in a million years?"

Mengeles started to laugh. His mother stuck her head out of the door that connected the kitchen with the garage.

"My two men sharing a joke? How nice. I just knew you'd get along!"

Roger opened his mouth, but no words came out. He wanted to say something to her, to make her realize what was really happening. But the older man was right. There was nothing he could say.

His mother's head disappeared as she returned to her coffee.

Mengeles' smile would have put a Cheshire cat to shame. "As my boss, Dread, might put it," he remarked with a chuckle, "Roger, my boy, you have been dealt with."

Roger stood there, unable to move, as if the confusion

of the last few minutes had tied his muscles in impossible knots. What could he do?

He had the terrible feeling that Mengeles was right. Without the Decoder Rings, he was trapped on Earth forever. He would never see Delores again—assuming, of course, that Delores was still alive.

And he would never know who, or what, the Plotmaster was.

THRILLS!

CHILLS!

SHOCKS!

YOCKS!

Will Roger ever see Delores again?
Will Doctor Dread triumph?
Is this the end of the Cineverse as we know it?
What else is Big Bertha hiding under that sarong?

DON'T MISS
OUR NEXT EXCITING CHAPTER:
BRIDE OF THE SLIME MONSTER!
Coming soon to a bookstore in YOUR neighborhood!